Deadly Odds

"Captain Hays and Captain Perez," Garcia called out in perfect English. "Throw down your weapons and surrender or be overwhelmed by my superior forces!"

In equally perfect Spanish, Jack Hays's normally quiet voice boomed out to his men. "Ready your weapons!"

Sands and the rest of the company answered with a chorus of cocking hammers.

"So be it!" Garcia reined his gray mount about, then called over his shoulder, "No quarter!"

"Hold your fire until my signal!" Jack called. "Let them get . . ."

Jack's words were drowned by a roaring cry that went up from Garcia's soldiers as they charged.

Ninety yards, Sands estimated the distance between him and the attacking Mexicans. *Seventy yards . . .*

Also in THE TEXIANS series from Pinnacle Books

THE TEXIANS #3

WAR DEVILS
ZACH WYATT

PINNACLE BOOKS NEW YORK

This is a work of fiction. All the characters and events portrayed in this book are fictional, and any resemblance to real people or incidents is purely coincidental.

THE TEXIANS #3: WAR DEVILS

An original Pinnacle Books edition, published for the first time anywhere.

First printing/December 1984

ISBN: 0-523-42221-0

Can. ISBN: 0-523-43213-5

Printed in the United States of America

PINNACLE BOOKS, INC.
1430 Broadway
New York, New York 10018

9 8 7 6 5 4 3 2 1

For fellow Texian Larry McNeely

☆ ONE ☆

Death sat at Josh Sands's right elbow. And left. To conceal the nervous bobble of his Adam's apple, the lanky Texian ran a hand over the dense beard sprouted on his face. His gaze shifted to stare into Death's cold black eyes as he accepted the pipe passed to him.

For an instant Sands's attention focused on the thin stream of blue tobacco smoke that curled from the gourd bowl cupped in his palms, then he placed the long reed stem to his lips and sucked in deeply. Holding the calming smoke in his lungs for a pounding heartbeat, he exhaled and handed the pipe to his left.

Armpits sticky with sweat, his eyes lifted to once again meet Death's gaze—Death's seven emotionless stares. For Death was not a single entity, but seven Comanche braves sitting cross-legged in a tight circle about a smoldering fire or dried mesquite and buffalo chips. The fire burned in the middle of a shadowy tipi made claustrophobic by stagnant layers of heavy smoke that refused to rise and escape out the smoke hole at the top of the hide shelter.

Have I completely lost what little sense God gave me? *I've got no business being here,* Sands's doubts assailed him. He felt a rivulet of sweat trickle through the hairs of his chest, uncertain whether it was from the tipi's stifling heat or his own unrest.

The six-shot Colt, tucked securely in his belt at the small of his back and concealed by the loose buckskin jacket he wore, felt as useless as the brace of single-shot pistols and hunting knife that had been stripped from him and left outside on the ground before he had been allowed to enter the council tipi. Still, he told himself, he did have the Colt just in case—his hole card.

A snow-haired old brave wearing a face like bullhide cracked from improper curing tapped a mound of gray ash from the gourd pipe and refilled it with hand-crushed tobacco from a beaded pouch slung at his waist. Placing a thin twig into the fire's embers, the ancient warrior held it there until the wood ignited, then touched the burning sliver to the fresh bowl. He was called Coyote Speaks, civil leader for this small *Pehnahterkuh* Comanche band. The pipe was the seventh he had filled, lit, and passed to the others gathered in his tipi, all without a single word.

Sands sucked at his cheeks and worked his tongue in an attempt to draw saliva into a mouth left cotton-dry by the pipe's six predecessors. He forced himself to remain calm and patient. The sharing of tobacco and the silence formed intricate parts of the council. Both, the Comanche believed, allowed a man to clear his mind in preparation for discussing matters of importance.

Palavering with braves is no place for a ranger, Sands thought as the realization of what he was doing brought gooseflesh rippling up and down his back. For a young man who had fought the lords of the plains since turning fifteen, he felt naked and estranged this close to Comanche braves without pistols and rifle in hand. He was an Indian fighter, a ranger . . .

Sands caught himself. He was no longer a ranger—hadn't been for two months now. If he had still been with Captain John Coffee Hays's ranging company in San Antonio, he wouldn't be here now, hidden beneath his bushy, full beard and wide-brimmed sombrero, looking like some Comanchero come to barter with the *Pehnahterkuh*. And all for a fifty-fifty split of two hundred dollars.

But then, that was the image he wanted to present to the Comanche band. One he carefully cultivated by only speaking Spanish and keeping his Colt concealed beneath his jacket. A single glimpse of the six-shot .34 caliber pistol and the braves would have him pegged. No others within the Republic of Texas presently carried the pistols from Paterson, New Jersey. That he hadn't raised his guns against the *Pehnahterkuh* for two months would make no difference to these braves. Ten minutes after they caught sight of the Colt, he would likely be staked naked atop a red ant hill, his body coated in honey.

Sonofabitchin' politicians, he silently cursed the Texas Congress in Austin. Their lack of understanding had severed his ties with the rangers. *Stupid bastards don't know their backsides from* . . .

He edged the unspoken bitterness away. No politician had brought him so far into Comancheria. He had come on his own free will—not to fight the Comanche, but to save the life of a three-year-old girl.

Sands accepted the pipe and once more inhaled the tobacco smoke. His eyes drifted from Coyote Speaks to the black man seated at the leader's right, Benjamin Franklin Webb, Sands's partner in this venture. The former slave stood an inch under Sands's own six feet, although his muscular frame looked twice as wide as Sands's own lanky body. He had no idea of Ben's age, but the hint of gray at the man's temples bespoke maybe two decades separating him from Sands's own twenty-three years.

Without Ben's presence, Sands would never have made it to this small camp beside the Colorado River. No man with skin pigmentation lighter than Ben's blue-black could have come so deep into Comanche territory and kept his scalp. But a black man could wander the plains without drawing more than a passing glance from the Comanche bands.

"A man without a soul" was the Comanche description of a Negro. For the *Nermernuh,* "the People," as the savage lords of the plains called themselves, there was no niche in their concept of the universe for black-skinned men, whom they had only encountered since settlers began immigrating into Texas. While they could not deny the existence of black men, they found it simpler to give blacks the status of beings who were real yet unreal, rather than reweave the thread of their traditional myths to make a place for Negroes in the world.

Since a black man was a nonentity, the Comanches had nothing to fear from him, and they made no attempt to thwart his incursions into Comanche lands. So it was that Ben, aided by Sands's own disguise, was able to lead them to this parlay without inviting Indian attack.

It was directly to Ben that Coyote Speaks now turned and in his native tongue said, "I have pondered your offer since you came from out of the rising sun two days past. The young child that you seek is now a member of Forty Horses' family and dwells in his tipi as his daughter."

Sands caught himself before his gaze shifted to the young naked-chested warrior to Coyote Speaks's left. To have done so might have given away the fact he spoke Comanche. He also repressed an inward reaction that was somewhere between an icy shiver and a sigh of relief.

Sally Ann Qayle, the three-year-old Comanche captive they sought, had been adopted and was now considered a *Pehnahterkuh*, which meant she had not suffered the tortures normally reserved for the *Nermernuh*'s captives. From that came Sands's relief.

That she was now Forty Horses' daughter brought icy fear. Twenty scalps hung at the entrance to the warrior's tipi, more gruesome trophies than Sands had seen displayed on any other of the Comanche dwellings. Those scalps bespoke Forty Horses' courage as a war chief and the respect in which he was held among this small band of fourteen tipis. Such a brave was not likely to give up a daughter, even an adopted white child, without causing trouble.

"After long hours of council with the men of our band, Forty Horses has decided to accept your offer. He will now go and get the child," Coyote Speaks continued as he turned to Forty Horses, nodded, then glanced back to Ben. "You will get the horses and mules."

No sign of acceptance was on Forty Horses' face when he pushed from the ground with a grunt and stood scowling down at the council. His countenance lacked the Comanche black and red paints, but Sands easily imagined the young warrior's face streaked in the colors of war, screaming in fury from behind a war lance aimed directly at a white man's chest.

With another displeased grunt, Forty Horses pivoted on

the balls of his moccasined feet, ducked low, threw back the tipi's flap, and stormed out of the council. Sands quietly released a sigh of relief. The huffed grunts and scowl were far less than he had expected from the warrior.

It was Ben Webb who spoke now, in Spanish, telling Sands to get the mules and horses they had brought from San Antonio to trade for the Qayle girl. Sands nodded, muttered, *"Si,"* and rose to follow Forty Horses from the smoke-filled buffalo-hide tent.

Outside, he drew a deep breath to clear his lungs and head while he glanced about the Comanche camp. This band of *Pehnahterkuh* Comanches *was* small. Once its camp might have swelled with as many as a hundred tipis. Now it consisted of a mere fourteen tents. The defeat of the war chief Buffalo Hump and his *Nermernuh* army at the Battle of Plum Creek had scattered the Honey-Eater bands and left the southernmost division of the Comanche nation little more than a skeleton of its former self.

Only a matter of months ago the *Pehnahterkuh* had terrorized the Texas frontier. Now it was the northern bands, the *Tehnawa*, and *Tahneemuh*, and the aloof *Kwerharrehnuh* that led war parties against white settlers.

Sands's gaze made a full circuit around the camp. If the remaining members of the tiny village knew or cared about the council in Coyote Speaks's tipi, he found no indication of it. Squaws worked before their tipis, preparing the noon meals while older men too ancient to be considered braves sat on the ground, chipping flint into arrow- and spear-heads or simply basking in the spring sun. The Comanche children were playing like children anywhere.

A piercing, frightened dog's yap spun Sands around. He shuddered as he saw an old squaw with a mesquite club in her right hand and the limp body of a dead mongrel dog dangling from her left as she walked from behind a tipi. Without a glance to the rest of the camp, she seated herself beside a small camp fire, drew a hunting knife from a scabbard at her waist, and began to dress the dead animal.

Now Sands understood Forty Horses' lack of protest over the trading of his adopted daughter. Dog meat, like fish and fowl, was taboo to the Comanches. Only in times of starvation did the Indians partake of taboo meats.

The winter had been hard for Coyote Speaks's *Pehnahterkuh* band; there was no other reason for the squaws to be slaughtering the camp's dogs. The three mules, coffee, corn meal, and flour Ben and he had brought would help feed the small band until the great buffalo herds migrated southward.

Turning from the grisly butcher, Sands hastened to the east side of the camp and the three mules and four horses staked out there. Two of the horses were Ben's and his own mounts, the remainder of the animals and the heavy-laden packs they carried were a father's ransom for a three-year-old daughter who had been stolen from him in a Comanche raid that had taken the life of his wife and only son.

There was no greater wealth than horses for a Comanche. And the *Pehnahterkuh*, like most bands, preferred mule meat to that of wild and stringy longhorn cattle. The packs were stuffed, straining their rope bindings with foodstuffs, vermilion, cloth, mirrors, and ten Bibles.

Sally Ann Qayle was all that remained of Jess Qayle's family. The stock, trade goods, and two hundred dollars awaiting Ben and Sands when they returned the child to her father was the total of the farmer's worldly wealth.

That Sands was no longer a ranger did not diminish the importance of what he did this day for the farmer who was attempting to rebuild a life rent asunder by a Comanche Blood Moon raid.

Gathering the animals' shanks and reins, Sands led Jess Qayle's ransom back to Coyote Speaks's tipi. Ben and the council stood waiting for him, as did Forty Horses with the young girl clutched in his bare arms.

Sally Ann was smaller than Sands expected. Nor did she bear any signs of abuse, but then Sands didn't expect to see any. She was Forty Horses' adopted daughter, and to a Comanche that was the same as being born of *Nermernuh* blood.

Her soiled buckskin dress and a face smudged with grease and dirt could not hide her vulnerable beauty. Her wide, frightened eyes and the soft brown of her hair gave the child the appearance of a newborn fawn. Sands could easily understand Jess Qayle's willingness to sacrifice all he owned to reclaim his daughter.

Taking the three mules and two horses from Sands, Coyote Speaks led them to Forty Horses and accepted Sally Ann from the scowling warrior. The band's civil leader then passed the girl to Ben.

"The child is yours now. We have no further need to talk."

With that, the ancient leader turned and entered his tipi. A moment later the rest of the council dispersed, leaving Ben and Sands staring into Forty Horses' hate-filled face. Displaying the same brusqueness with which he had left the council, the warrior turned his back on the two Texians and strode away.

"We'd best get the hell out of here," Sands said to his partner in Spanish.

Ben nodded, then to the girl, who whimpered softly in his arms, he said, "No need to cry, little one. Tomorrow eve'n' old Ben's going to return you to your daddy's arms. Everything's going to be all right. Going to be all right."

"Daddy?" the girl asked, sniffling back the tears that rolled from her round brown eyes.

"That's right!" Ben grinned widely as he eased into the saddle, his young ward cradled in a massive arm. "We're going home to your daddy. All we've got to do is ride south for a piece, then you'll be with your daddy. Then every little thing will be just fine."

Ben's gentle words might have brought comfort to Sally Ann, but they did nothing to ease the niggling doubt at the back of Sands's mind. Swinging astride his mount, he nudged the bay gelding toward the south and San Antonio. As former ranger and black freedman rode from the Comanche tipis, Sands glanced back over his shoulder. At the opposite end of the camp, Forty Horses stood glaring at their departure.

☆ TWO ☆

Ben Webb blinked and rubbed at his eyes as Sands nudged his partner from a snore that sounded like a two-handed saw biting into green pine. "Mornin' already? What time is it anyway? Feels like I just bundled up in these old blankets."

"Sun'll be up in a minute or two—about seven, I'd guess." Sands handed the ex-slave a tin cup of steaming, pan-boiled coffee then pulled a pocket watch from his buckskin breeches. His thumb ran over the cover's engraving of an English gentleman on a fox hunt before opening it. "Seven exactly."

"Hmmm." Ben blew at the steam rising from the cup, then sipped gingerly at the scalding brew. "Josh, there's something I've been wantin' to ask you. Why were all them Bibles packed in the goods we traded for little Sally Ann? Comanches haven't all of a sudden got religion, have they?"

Sands chuckled. "Anything but that. They want the paper for their war shields. Those thin sheets the Good Word is printed on are perfect for stuffing between the two layers of leather they use for shields. Works a lot better than grass and twigs. Been known to deflect rifle balls."

11

"Mmmm. This is mighty good . . ." Abruptly Ben's eyes went white and round as saucers and rolled questioningly to Sands. "Coffee? You got a fire going? I thought we was cold camping?"

Sands placed a finger to his lips, signaling Ben to keep his voice down, then tilted his head to the three-year-old girl still asleep beneath two blankets beside a low flickering campfire.

"No need for a cold camp if the Comanches already know where you are," Sands answered while he squatted by the fire and poured himself a cup of coffee. "Wish we had some milk or something to give her when she wakes. Coffee and jerky ain't a fittin' breakfast for a child."

"Already know where we are?" Ben's eyes went even rounder. His head jerked from side to side, searching the rocky terrain about them. "You mean we've got bucks on our tail?"

"Just beyond that rise to the south." Sands indicated with a tilt of his sombreroed head. "Caught a glimpse of one about an hour before the moon went down. I heard horses before that—at least three. Could be more."

"They stayin' 'way 'cause of me?" Ben took a deep drink from the cup, his gaze straying back to the southern rise.

Sands shook his head as he stood and walked to the saddlebags lying beside his bedroll and pulled out a leather pouch from which he extracted a twist of jerked beef. "It's the girl keeping them back."

"Sally Ann?" Ben asked as he caught the pouch Sands tossed to him. "Why'd a little girl keep 'em away?"

"Unless I'm way off course, that's Forty Horses out there with a couple of his friends." Sands tore a bite from a strip of dried, salted, and peppered beef, working the hard meat between his teeth.

"Forty Horses? No reason for him to come chasing after us. He accepted the trade." Ben gnawed at his own twist of jerky.

"That was yesterday when the camp needed food. Today Coyote Speaks's band has a belly full of mule, and Forty Horses wants his daughter back." Sands washed the stringy jerky down with coffee. "It's Comanches we're dealing with here. It would be quite a coup if Forty Horses could steal Sally Ann back. A red man's sense of honor and fair play are different from a white man's."

"I lived half my life chained by the white man's fair play," Ben said with a contemptuous grunt.

Sands ignored his partner's comment. He wasn't in the mood to discuss the morality of slavery. That was something better left to politicians who relished ranting and raving over such issues. For him slavery was simply a fact of life—today it existed, tomorrow it might not. Either way it didn't affect his life. Neither he nor his family, when they had been alive, had ever been rich enough to own slaves.

Ben's eyes rolled back to the rise. "What do we do now?"

"Finish our breakfast and act as though we don't know they're out there." Sands squatted on his heels beside Ben and traced a jagged semicircle in the sand with a fingertip. "This is Balcones Escarpment."

On the northwest side of the semicircle he drew a snaking line. "And this is the San Saba River. Coyote Speaks's band was camped here." He drew an X below Balcones Escarpment. "That's San Antonio. And we're here." His fingertip dug into the sand halfway between the

San Saba and the frontier town. "We pressed our horses yesterday and covered about seventy-five miles by riding late into the night. That leaves us with another seventy-five miles."

"We could ride hard again," Ben suggested.

"Yep—and we'd ride our mounts right into the ground," Sands answered with a disapproving shake of his head. "Think we'd better take it slow and easy. Besides, we ain't certain Forty Horses has come to take the girl back. Comanches are mighty particular when it comes to their children, even adopted ones. A lot of whites could take parentin' lessons fom them. Maybe he just wants to make sure we get Sally Ann home safely."

"And maybe a brave recognized you as one of Jack Hays's rangers."

"Maybe . . . maybe not." Sands's money was on the "not." If he had been recognized, they would have never been permitted to leave the Comanche camp. "But as long as they're out there, leaving us alone, we act like we don't even know they're there. Now finish your coffee while I saddle the horses. Soon as you're done, wake the girl and feed her so we can get a move on."

Ben nodded and took another gulp from the cup as his gaze once more returned to the rise.

One instant there were only long fingery shadows stretching out from the break of scrub cedars into the shallow valley of two opposing hogback ridges. Then, in the blinking of an eye, shadows stood within the shadows.

Sands stared directly at the cedars, then watched them from the corner of an eye. The two riders cloaked in the darkening shade were no mirage or illusion created by the rapidly setting sun. They were real, and they were Comanche.

Just as real were the two mounted braves who waited beside an eroded outthrust of limestone at the foot of the opposite ridge. And the two riders now openly keeping pace on the crests of the two hogbacks.

"Tell me I'm seeing things," Ben said softly as his head turn from side to side. "Tell me those aren't two bucks parading on each side of us."

"There's four more ahead," Sands replied, his mind playing through a hundred possibilities, each darker than the one before. "And sneak a gander behind us. I think I can make out the hooves of another two horses."

Ben did. "Three horses—Comanches just riding slow and steady as though they don't care who sees 'em."

"They don't. They want us to see them. Want us to make a move." *Three behind, two to the side, and four ahead*, Sands tallied up the odds. Nine was a far cry from the three he had estimated this morning. "Now all we've got to do is figure out what move they want us to make— and not make it."

"Do we run for it?" Ben's right hand eased to one of the two single-shot pistols he carried.

Sands leaned toward the young passenger who sat in front of Ben in the saddle. Sally Ann Qayle's head lay nestled against the former slave's chest. Her eyes were sleepy slits. It had been a long day for the child, and an equally long day for the two horses. Sands estimated they had covered fifty miles since the morning—fifty hard miles.

"If it were just you and me, I'd say dig in spurs and burn 'em with powder." Sands's gaze wandered over the valley, seeking, searching. "But that's exactly what I think they want us to do."

A charge forward and they would face four braves who might return the attack. But in all likelihood the warriors would simply wheel their mustangs, wait for Ben and him to pass, then turn their backs into pin cushions with a volley of arrows. After all, why endanger the child's life with a head-on attack when arrows could do the job so neatly?

Should they try an escape by riding down on the three behind, Sands expected the Comanches would also wheel and wait for them to pass before unleashing their arrows. As for the hogbacks, that would be insanity, suicide. Both were far too steep for the horses to climb at more than a leisurely walk. Before Ben or he could make it to either one of the crests, the braves before and behind would be on them.

"Then what'd ya have in mind?" Ben's voice was steeped in doubt.

"They've got us boxed in." Sands was as uncertain as Ben. "There's only one thing we can do—make a stand." He nodded to three gnarled live oaks ahead. The scrawny trees offered little cover, but the limestone boulders they grew beside would provide protection to the south and east.

"Make a stand . . ." Ben mumbled, his head shaking. Then he nodded a reluctant acceptance. "If that's the only way you see."

"That's all I can see," Sands answered. "Ride up to those oaks as though nothing's wrong. The second you reach them, swing down and tie your mare to a branch. We'll have to use our horses for cover. The oaks just aren't enough."

"Which means, if we make it through this, odds are we'll be walking the rest of the way back to San Antonio," Ben said, glancing at his Comanchero-disguised partner, a pained expression twisting his features.

Sands didn't answer the obvious. As much as Comanches prized horses, they would have no qualms about killing two mounts to get at their riders—and Jess Qayle's daughter.

"Here goes nothing." Ben abruptly reined his horse toward the three oaks.

Sands was at his heels. Together the two men wrenched rifles from saddle holsters, swung from the saddle, and tied their mounts to twisted branches.

"Best get her back among the boulders." Sands glanced at Sally Ann, whose wide eyes darted about with uncertainty now.

Ben nodded and pulled his bedroll from the back of his saddle. Seconds later he deposited his ward on the ground against the apex formed by the limestone boulders.

"Little darlin', we've got some men following us who want to play hide and seek." Ben's voice was playfully light as he smiled down at the child. "We're going to hide you here under these blankets. You keep real quiet now so they won't find you. Understand?"

"Yes," the girl answered, returning his smile.

"Good. Don't make even a little peep, no matter what happens," Ben said as he covered the girl with his bedroll.

"Put these around her," Sands said, then tossed his partner the saddles off their mounts.

Ben carefully placed the saddles on either side of the covered child. "Guess that's the best we can do."

Sands glanced at the hidden girl. Boulders protected her on two sides and saddles to the north and west. If it came to shooting, at least she had a good chance of surviving even if the two men who had come to rescue her from her Comanche kidnappers didn't.

"Josh, looks like we've got their attention." Ben's head nodded toward the three riders who had trailed behind them.

With a quick check on the other six braves, who remained motionless, Sands looked back to the north. One rider reined his mount toward the stand of oaks, then stopped fifty yards from the men.

"I have come for my daughter Antelope Runs." It was Forty Horses who spoke. "Return her to me and you may keep your lives. Refuse and your scalps shall hang from my tipi."

Sands whispered to Ben, "He hasn't come to kill. He's without war paint. When they attack, they'll be hesitant. Forty Horses doesn't want to hurt the child."

"I await your answer," the warrior called out.

Drawing a deep, steadying breath, Sands stepped from between the cover of the two horses and faced the brave. In broken Comanche, he said, "You have taken the horses, mules, and food of the child's true father. Now you come to steal her back to your tipi. Is there no honor among the Honey-Eaters? Or have the Kiowas named you correctly—Comanche, the snake that runs backward? The child must be returned to her father."

"Antelope Runs has but one father, and he is Forty Horses," the warrior called out his reply. "And you have chosen to die. I will respect that choice. Ay-ay-ay-ay-aieeeeeeeee!"

The doglike yapping tearing from his lips, Forty Horses' heels rose and drove down to dig into the flanks of the pinto mustang he sat astride. Forty Horses leveled the muzzle of his rifle at Sands as his horse bolted forward in a dead run.

The former ranger reacted instinctively. Throwing himself to the right, Sands hit the sandy ground in a roll as the Comanche's rifle spat forth its lead ball in a thunderous explosion of black powder. A hot whine sizzled by Sands's head. The high-pitched scream of death abruptly ended in a hollow thud as the rifle ball slammed harmlessly into the ground where Sands had stood but a heartbeat before.

While Sands sought to swing his own long rifle into play, another rifle barked from behind him as Ben answered Forty Horses' attack in kind.

The warrior's body jerked rigid, and his rifle flew from his hands to fall to the ground as the former slave's ball struck home. But Forty Horses did not fall. Instead, he threw himself low to the paint's neck and wheeled about in retreat.

"Damn!" Ben railed. "I only nicked his shoulder. I was aiming for his chest!"

"You cost him his—"

Sands's words were drowned in the bloodcurdling cries of seven Comanche warriors. Forty Horses had rejoined his two companions, and they charged together—as did the four braves who had waited motionless at the head of the valley.

☆ THREE ☆

Shoving to his feet, Sands swirled and ducked back behind the protection of the two horses. From his belt, he pulled a brace of single-shot pistols and passed them to Ben, who now leaned his expended rifle against the trunk of an oak and reached for his own pistols.

"That'll give you four shots. With luck we can make 'em think both of us are carrying Colts," Sands said, drawing his revolver from the holster now hanging at his waist. "I'll take the four."

With a nod, Ben thumbed back the hammers to Sands's two pistols as he turned to meet Forty Horses and his two charging companions. Sands moved to the boulders, placed his Colt within easy reach atop one, and lifted his rifle to yank back its hammer.

Their dog-imitating cries tearing from chest and throat, and their raven black hair trailing wildly behind them, the four braves urged their mustangs forward in a wild run. That Sands had faced a hundred similar charges since a Comanche war party had attacked his family's supply store when he was but a boy of nine did nothing to lessen the ice floe that crept along his spine while he stared into the warriors' faces, visages of death grotesquely twisted with hate and blood lust.

21

Nor did their terrible presence leave him frozen with fear. His blue-gray eyes coursed over the four as he firmly nestled the rifle's stock into the hollow of his shoulder. Only one of the four barreling down from the head of the valley carried a rifle. Two raised bows with arrows notched, and the remaining warrior hefted a war lance with two eagle feathers aswirl beneath its flint tip.

Sands's sight fell on the brave armed with the rifle. Centering on the warrior's chest, his finger curled around the trigger and squeezed. With a metallic click, the hammer dropped and black powder exploded in a rolling blast and a billowing dark cloud.

Sands didn't wait for the haze to clear to check the accuracy of his aim. Instead, he cast the now useless rifle aside and hefted the Colt in his right hand. When he looked again, only three braves yowled down on him. The fourth, rifle half-buried in the sand, lay dead or dying on the ground.

Thumb now edging back the pistol's hammer, Sands's forefinger curled about the trigger. Ill-balanced it was, and its .34 caliber far too light for the needs of a man in the wilds of Texas, but the Colt brought something to the frontier that was beyond the ability of any other pistol—six shots!

Sands sighted on a brave astride a dappled roan mustang as the Comanche pulled back the gut string of his bow. His finger squeezed the trigger, which once more receded into the pistol as the hammer fell.

Again the former ranger didn't wait to view the effect of his shot. This time he ducked to avoid the whistling shaft that the brave had released the instant before the shot. A woody thud of flint driving into green oak came from behind him—as did the bark of Ben's pistols.

"Sonofabitch!" Sands cursed as he rose, recocking the Colt.

Three braves still urged their horses down toward the boulders—his shot had been wild! He aimed and fired again, again. Behind him, Ben's reports came like an echo.

Sands squeezed off another shot, then dropped behind the limestone again as a Comanche arrow whined toward him. There was no thud of flint and wood this time, but the frightened snort of a horse.

Sands's gaze darted over his shoulder. A thin trace of crimson ran across the rump of Ben's chestnut mare where the arrow's head had grazed across her sleek coat. Inwardly, Sands sighed with relief. The wound was no more than a scratch—it could have been death.

"I got one," Ben spat through clenched teeth as he peered through the foglike cloud of smoke about him. Then bewilderment brought a stutter to his voice. "Wha—wha—what's going on? They're turning tail!"

Pushing from his knees, Sands peered over the boulder. Two of the four Comanches who had begun the charge from the head of the valley were indeed wheeling their mustangs about in retreat. The other two lay dead in the sand.

"Reload!" That single word came harsh and rasping from Sands's dry mouth. "They'll be back."

Ben didn't question the order but retrieved powder and lead balls from his saddlebags while Sands broke the Colt down into its three sections, placed fresh charges in its cylinder, then reloaded his rifle. Both men immediately turned to face another charge. None came.

"They're gone!" Ben said as he searched the valley.

"Even the braves on the ridge are gone. Think we drove 'em off?"

"Not likely." Sands's own gaze ran over the valley and the two hogbacks, finding no trace of Forty Horses and his war party, except the bodies of the three cut down in the charge. "We surprised them with our firepower. They're still out there, licking their wounds, deciding what to do next. But they'll be back."

When ranger Captain Jack Hays had first introduced the six-shot Colts to the frontier, the Comanche had been terrified of the new weapons that spat death so readily. That terror had lasted for only a couple of months, and then the *Nermernuh* adjusted and accepted the revolver for what it was—simply another gun.

Sands knew he had caught Forty Horses off guard with the hidden Colt and had cost the warrior more men than he expected to lose. When the brave returned, he would be prepared. "They'll probably wait for dark, before the moon's up, to come back."

"Sneakin' in here on foot, makin' no more sound than the breeze," Ben added.

Sands sucked in a deep breath. "If I were Forty Horses, that's what I'd do. He and his braves can belly-crawl, quiet as snakes in this sand. In the darkness, they can be on us without . . ."

His words trailed into silence. Dwelling on what would happen if they remained here offered no comfort. If they intended to see another sunrise, they had to be out of the oaks before Forty Horses returned.

"Best check on Sally Ann." Sands tilted his head toward the bundled child who had remained totally silent during the attack.

"I'll be damned," Ben said with a shake of his head as he crossed to the child and edged back the blankets. "She's sound asleep. How in hell can she sleep at a time like this—when half the Comanche Nation is after our hair?"

Sands smiled as he glanced toward the sleeping child. He shrugged and said, "We covered a lot of ground today, she was tired. Let her sleep. It's best she doesn't know what's happening."

While Ben gently replaced the bedroll, Sands's attention returned to the valley, searching the now empty hogbacks. The seed of an idea began to sprout in his head.

"Damn! Look what the red-skinned bastards went and did to my Louisville Lady," Ben said, standing by his chestnut mare, a pained grimace contorting his face while he examined the bloody graze on the horse's rump.

"It's only a scratch," Sands answered, his voice sharp with irritation. "Lucky the arrow didn't hit lower."

"Scratch? Only a scratch?" Ben turned and stared at his partner in disbelief. "This here's a pure-blooded Kentucky thoroughbred! She'd cost a man five hundred Yankee dollars in auction. Ain't no such thing as just a scratch on a fine animal like this. Got to take prime care of this little darlin'. She's going to help make me a rich man."

Sands ignored the black man's comments. They were both lucky their horses weren't lying on the ground riddled with Comanche shafts. If Forty Horses hadn't been so concerned about Sally Ann, they would have been killed in the attack.

"Ten minutes and the sun will be down," Sands said as his gaze once more returned to the hogbacks. "Another twenty minutes and it'll be black as sin. That gives us half an hour to come up with something."

"Got any suggestions?" Ben rummaged in his saddle-bags and produced a tin of sulfur powder, which he sprinkled on the mare's wound.

"We've got two choices," Sands answered. "Stay here and fight . . . or make a run for it as soon as it gets dark."

"There's still braves at both ends of the valley," Ben replied with a nod fore and aft. "Not as many as before, but still enough to do us serious damage."

Sands sucked at his teeth. "The hogbacks are clear now. Soon as it's dark, Forty Horses is going to come belly-crawling in here. We could make a run then . . . up that slope." Sands pointed to the left. "Reckon it's a bit higher than the rest, but it's less steep. If our luck holds out we might, just might, be able to clear the crest before Forty Horses could catch us."

"Sounds a damned sight better than sitting here and waiting for them bucks to lift our scalps," Ben replied, and started toward the saddles. "I'll get the horses ready."

"Not yet." Sands reached out and grabbed his partner's arm, stopping him. "Forty Horses is eyeballing our every move. Don't want to give ourselves away. We'll wait until it's dark, give the braves time to start moving in. I want them as far away from their ponies as possible when we light out of here."

Ben paused as though considering all Sands had said, then replied, "Sounds like—"

He never finished the sentence. The yipping, high-pitched cries of the Comanches came from the head of the valley!

"What the hell?" Sands grabbed up his rifle and swung it in the direction of the war cries.

Why would Forty Horses attack now when there was still light? It didn't make sense. Yet from out of the gathering darkness, two braves drove their mustangs in a dead run toward the boulders.

"It don't make no sense, but it's quiet on this end," Ben said.

Sands glanced over his shoulder. The valley behind them was empty. "Watch the hogbacks! Forty Horses may try to ride down on us from both sides!"

The crack of gunshots jerked Sands's head back around in time to see one of the charging warriors tumble from the back of his pony. He blinked, uncertain if he believed what his eyes saw. Then he smiled.

Forty Horses' guards at the head of the valley weren't attacking. They were running—from eight mounted men who rode at their heels! White men with pistols ablaze.

Three sharp reports echoed through the valley. The remaining warrior jerked under the impact of hot lead, then slumped forward and rolled from the neck of his pony like a rag doll. He hit the sandy floor of the valley and lay there dead.

"Rangers!" Sands shouted as he turned to Ben with a wide grin splitting his face. "I don't know how, but those men are rangers!"

Ben turned, glanced at the approaching riders with uncertainty, then an ivory grin crept across his ebony face. "I'll be damned!"

"In time we probably both will! But not tonight!" Sands bounded atop the nearest boulder, lifted his wide-brimmed sombrero, and waved at the ranging company.

Seconds later the eight men reined to a halt beside the stand of three oaks. A soft-spoken voice came from the lead rider. "What's the situation here? We heard shooting. Anyone hurt?"

"We've still got our hair, Jack," Sands said, recognizing the familiar voice of ranger Captain John Coffee Hays. "Though for a while I had doubts about it being there tomorrow morning. There's a buck named Forty Horses and one other brave at the back of the valley who took a shining to it. Wants it hanging on a pole outside his tipi. Should be two more lurking about somewhere. Last we saw of them, they were atop these two hogbacks."

"Josh? Josh Sands?" Jack Hays squinted at Sands and rubbed a hand over his chin. "Is that you under all those whiskers?"

"One and the same!"

"Bejesus, what are you doing? I thought you were working at the Casa de Chavela." Jack shook his head, then turned to a man on his left. "Simpson, you heard the man! There's four bucks around here—what are you and the men waiting for?"

Simpson and the rest of Hays's company answered by digging their spurs into their mounts' flanks and riding toward the far end of the valley.

"Reckon they can handle four Comanches without getting into too much trouble." Hays watched his men's departure for a few moments, then turned back to Sands. "Now, suppose you explain what you're doing out here looking for an Indian haircut. I thought you were working in that cantina back in San Antonio."

Sands grinned. "It's a long story, Jack."

☆ FOUR ☆

While Ben and Sands saddled their horses, Jack Hays listened as they recounted how Jess Qayle had approached Sands in San Antonio two weeks ago.

"He has a farm between Gonzales and San Antonio. A Comanche war party attacked it about six weeks back, killed his wife and son, left him for dead with an arrow in his back," Sands explained.

"Qayle . . . Qayle," Jack mused aloud as he hooked his right knee over the broad horn of his saddle. "The name seems familiar, but I can't seem to place a face with it."

"He approached you before he sought me out." Sands tightened the cinch about his bay. "That war party also kidnapped his three-year-old baby daughter."

"Now I remember. Told him I'd do what I could, but not to expect much. Not with the cutbacks in my company," Jack said with a thoughtful nod. "I mentioned his daughter to my Lipan scouts, but they didn't come up with anything."

"He was afraid of that. When he heard there were some out-of-work rangers in San Antonio, he went looking for one." Sands slapped the gelding's stomach with an open palm and drew the girth in two more notches when the horse expelled the air it held in its lungs. "Qayle offered two hundred dollars if I returned his daughter to him. I accepted on the condition I could convince Ben to go along with me."

"Believe in weighting a hand in your favor, don't you?" Jack grinned and winked at Sands's partner.

"When I can," Sands replied with a chuckle.

Ben Webb's reputation was well-known along the frontier. In the past three years the former slave had made five ventures into Comancheria seeking wives, sons, and daughters taken captive in Comanche raids. On each occasion, he had returned with those he had gone after. Once he had brought out three additional captives, to the joy and relief of their families.

"Too bad you boys weren't successful this time." Jack pursed his lips and shook his head. "I've seen men hurtin' before, but Qayle was all pain. The loss of his family turned the world completely upside down for him."

"Captain." Ben drew Jack's attention, then walked to where his bedroll lay spread on the ground. Carefully, he picked up the corners of the blankets and lifted them enough for Hays to peek beneath.

"I'll be damned!" A soft whistle of admiration escaped the ranger captain's pursed lips a moment before his face split in a wide grin. "There's going to be one happy man when he sets his eyes on that little angel. You two ought to . . ."

Jack's head jerked around at the sound of approaching hooves. His ranger company rode in from the far end of the small valley. No prisoners or Indian ponies accompanied them.

"They pulled a slip on us, Capt'n," Bill Simpson said as the company reined to a halt beside Jack. "They lit out before we got to the end of the valley. Followed their tracks 'bout a mile to a swollen creek. Searched the banks a bit but couldn't find a trace. Figured they took to the water.''

"You did what you could. I can't ask for more than that," Jack said.

The worried furrows creasing Simpson's brow vanished, and the trace of a relieved smile touched the corners of his mouth. Sands saw the same appreciative smile on the faces of the rest of the company.

Another man might have cussed and berated the men for their failure, whether it was their fault or not. But other men were not John Coffee Hays. No matter what the situation, Jack always had the gift of the correct words to put his men at ease or fire their blood for battle.

Sands studied the young ranger captain, a mere year older than Sands himself. He felt no shame for the admiration he held for the man.

John Coffee Hays was a rarity among frontier men. Tennessee-born, Jack could only be described as a gentleman with impeccable manners—when the situation warranted. He was soft-spoken, with a voice that tended toward tenor rather than baritone; levelheaded, clear thinking, and calm, woe be the man who railed him enough to bring a hint of harshness to that soft voice. Jack never shouted; he acted before his voice ever rose that much in volume.

Slight in built and slim hipped, Jack Hays lacked the rugged appearance of a man who devoted his life to ranging the frontier. That exterior was deceptive: inside the ranger captain beat a heart as big as the republic he served—a heart utterly without fear.

Sands shook his head as he walked to where Sally Ann

lay asleep on the ground. Jack Hays was no talker, lacking the silver tongue possessed by politicians. Nor was he renowned for marksmanship. At least five out of every ten men were better with a pistol and rifle than the ranger captain. And no one had ever accused Jack of being an excellent horseman.

But not one man in a thousand had that certain indefinable something Hays possessed: he was a natural-born leader. When he spoke, men listened and followed, fully confident in the man's ability. And a ranger captain did lead—whether on routine patrol or into the heat of battle he was always at the head of his company.

Atop Jack's uncanny ability for sizing up his surroundings and circumstances in a matter of seconds and drawing valid conclusions, there was no better Indian fighter on the Texas frontier—or in the whole republic. Hays carefully studied the Apaches and Comanches, learned their tactics, then used those very tricks against the enemy.

Those in more civilized parts of the land might find Jack's approach to ranging brutal and cruel, Sands thought. But to those along the frontier, who lived in fear of their lives every time the full moon—the Blood Moon—rose, John Coffee Hays was a man revered for his quick thinking and quick action.

Easing back the blankets, Sands lifted Sally Ann from the ground and gently passed her up to Ben, who now sat astride his chestnut mare. Sands rerolled the blankets and tied them behind Ben's saddle before mounting his gelding.

"You two heading on toward Gonzales to return the child to her daddy?" Jack asked, glancing at Sands and Ben.

Sands shook his head. "San Antonio. Qayle's waiting for us at Barrett's boardinghouse."

"Good." Jack eased his mount eastward. "Reckon you won't mind a bit of company on the ride back."

"We'll welcome it, Capt'n," Ben answered as he reined beside Hays. "It's a long way back home, and there'll be a full moon up soon."

"Company's always welcomed," Sands agreed, glancing at Jack, whose face betrayed a frown. "What's the matter?"

"Just trying to piece a few words together," Jack replied.

"Trouble?" Sands asked.

"Yep. By the name of Agaton." Jack edged back the brim of his hat and scratched his head.

"The Mexican?" This from Ben. "Don't tell me he's come to San Antonio."

Agaton. Sands rolled the name around in his mind, placing the man with his deeds. Agaton headed a band of self-styled revolutionaries in northern Mexico. In truth, the man and his followers were no more than freebooters, brigands.

"If he'd come this far north, he wouldn't be a problem," Jack answered. "I'd have him locked away, waiting for the district judge to make his circuit. But rumor has it he's holed up down in Laredo."

"Long as he's in Laredo, there shouldn't be a problem," Sands said, realizing Hays was leaving out part of his story.

"That's the trouble; Agaton's crossed the border. He and his men attacked two traders out of San Antonio last week. Made off with two wagons laden with everything from hardware to tobacco."

Although relations between Mexico and Texas had been anything but friendly since the War of Independence, Sands was aware of the considerable trade that had sprung up along the border. Mexicans provided beans, sugar, flour, leather, shoes, and saddles in exchange for Texian calico, tobacco, and American hardware.

Hays paused, his gaze shifting between Ben and Sands. He drew a breath, then said, "I need men to ride south with me. Can't offer much in the way of pay—ten dollars a head—but it will be a change of scenery."

"Ten dollars!" Ben laughed so loudly that Sally Ann stirred in his arms and her eyes blinked open. Whispering the child back to sleep, he turned to Jack and in a low voice said, "You're offering me ten dollars to ride down to Laredo and maybe get my head shot off. Capt'n, I admit to being a bit touched. No man in his right mind would make a living ridin' into Comanche camps and tradin' them out of white captives. But I ain't *that* loco. The republic might claim Laredo, but it's still controlled by the Mexicans. The *alcalde* ain't goin' to appreciate you ridin' into his city and takin' away one of its upstandin' citizens in irons."

"No." Ben shook his head. "Unless you got an army ridin' with you, Capt'n Jack, I'm afraid you'll be going without Ben Webb. I got plans for this little mare of mine. And gettin' myself kilt for ten dollars ain't part of those plans."

"I've authorization for my company and four additional men," Jack said.

"Twelve men?" Ben's disbelief echoed Sands's own. "It's not me who's touched! You're going to ride into Laredo with twelve men?"

"Antonio Perez and thirteen of his men have volunteered to ride with me," Jack answered.

Captain Antonio Perez was one of San Antonio's well-known citizens and a daring Indian fighter. Having him along would add weight to the expedition south, but Sands still didn't like the odds.

"Perez and thirteen men, yourself and twelve men, that's still only twenty-seven." Sands bit at his lower lip thoughtfully. "Ben's right. You need an army with you. The Mexicans have troops in that area."

Even if Hays wanted an army with him, he was denied that option. The Republic of Texas was without an army, though it was badly needed.

Since Generalissimo Santa Anna's defeat at the Battle of San Jacinto and the winning of Texas' independence, ranger captains like Jack and the republic's military tacticians had warned that one day Mexico would attempt to reclaim her lost northern territory. She could do that by only one method—full military invasion.

Time and again the signs of a forthcoming invasion had flared. Mexican troops constantly crossed the Rio Grande to flaunt their colors in the face of Texian authority. Yet that feared and threatened invasion had never come. However, Sands, like every man and woman in the Republic of Texas, knew that one day the Mexican army would march northward and blood would flow.

Yet in spite of that constant threat from south of the border, Texas was still without an organized defense. The reason was simple—Texas couldn't afford a standing army.

Young and poor, the republic had disbanded its regular militia, only keeping a few token officers and men when Sam Houston assumed the office of president for a second time. The republic's coffers lacked the funds to outfit and maintain an army, let alone pay soldiers. Or rangers.

"Am I to take that as a no?" Jack glanced at Sands. "I'd've thought you'd jump at the chance to be ranging again."

Sands repressed the bitterness that seethed within his chest and swallowed the words writhing angrily on his tongue. Jack Hays wasn't responsible for his release from the rangers two months ago. The same lack of money that had forced the disbanding of the army had resulted in Hays's company being cut from twenty-five men to ten.

Men with families had been retained, the others let go. Sands had no family—except the rangers. The dismissal was like abruptly being disowned by every blood relative he had on the face of the earth. No, his bitterness was not directed at Jack Hays, but at the politicians in Austin who appropriated funds for the development of Texas commerce, yet lacked the insight to realize that a Mexican invasion could mean the end of this infant nation, that as long as Comanches ravaged the frontier, Texas would have no westward expansion.

"I'm not saying no . . . or yes. I need time to ponder the offer a bit," Sands finally answered, unable to escape the twinge of guilt in his breast, guilt that stemmed from his loyalty to Texas, the rangers, and Jack Hays. A loyalty that Texas did not return.

Or is it just a matter of bruised pride? Sands wasn't sure.

Money, the ridiculous ten dollars, was of little concern to Sands. He had often ranged with Hays when the republic somehow overlooked paying for the services of their rangers. Besides, he had more than five hundred dollars tucked away in a San Antonio bank: money remaining from the sale of a small herd of horses he had been given after the battle of Plum Creek.

It came down to whether he was willing to ride with the rangers again after his unceremonious dismissal—and then for only a few weeks at most. When Hays's company returned from Laredo, if they returned, he'd be back where he was right now—which was nowhere.

"Take all the time you need to ponder," Jack said. "But if you're going with me and the boys, you'd best make up your mind by noon tomorrow. That's when we're riding south. Not that I want to rush you."

Sands shook his head. "Thanks for giving a man so much consideration."

The three and the troop behind them fell silent as they rode eastward toward San Antonio. Overhead a cloudless summer sky was alive with a myriad of diamond-sparkling stars and a rising full moon.

☆ FIVE ☆

Uninhibited and unashamed tears rolled down Jess Qayle's cheeks as he stood in the parlor of Barrett's boardinghouse and tightly hugged his daughter to his breast. That it was a quarter past midnight and Sally Ann still wore her buffalo-hide dress and Comanche grease was of no concern to her father. All that mattered was that they had been reunited.

The farmer's tears were contagious. Within seconds, little Sally Ann sobbed as she clung to Jess's thin neck. Beside them, in nightdress and flannel robe, the boarding-house's proprietor, Netty Barrett, used the hem of her robe's sleeve to dab at the moisture trickling from the corners of her eyes.

Even Ben Webb was sniffling at the obvious love and joy of the father and daughter reunion. Sands glanced at his partner in disbelief, but found it difficult to see him through the moist blur of his own eyes.

When at last the tears and the hugs and the kisses subsided, Qayle passed Sally Ann into Netty's open arms. The rotund white-haired woman cuddled and crooned to the child while Qayle hastened from the parlor. He returned seconds later to place small pouches in both Ben's and Sands's hands.

"Five twenty-dollar gold pieces each ain't enough to pay for what you two did." Qayle's voice was still choked and tight, his eyes red from weeping. "Ain't nothing ever going to be able to pay you for bringing Sally Ann back to me. If there's ever anything I can do for either one of you—anything—you just call on me. Understand?"

"Mister Qayle," Ben said as he slipped his pouch into a pocket, "these are fair wages. A man can't ask for more than that."

"Ain't enough." Qayle shook his head with determination and ran a hand through straw-colored hair. "I mean it. If you need anything, call on me."

"We'll do that, Jess," Sands said, feeling relief when the man smiled, nodded, and turned back to take his daughter into his arms.

"He's right," Netty Barrett spoke up. "I'd like to show my appreciation for what you've done. If you two boys'll give me time to get the stove lit, I'll see if I can rustle you up some food that will put some meat on your bones."

"I'll camp in this parlor all night for that, Mrs. Barrett." Ben's head bobbed eagerly as he grinned his acceptance.

"And you, Josh Sands?" Netty asked.

The Widow Barrett was renowned in San Antonio for her cooking, and her offer was a promised feast that Sands was sorely tempted to accept. However, he shook his head. " 'Fraid I'll have to pass this time, Netty. Told Jack Hays I'd meet with him and share a steak."

The meeting with Hays was a lie, one that drew a raised eyebrow from the boardinghouse proprietor, but no verbal questioning, for which Sands was grateful. Saying his good-byes, he left Qayle still holding his daughter and

Ben with his mouth watering as Netty trooped into her kitchen to prepare the promised reward.

Sands's own reward came ten minutes later when he tied his bay gelding to a hitching rail outside the Casa de Chavela and entered the cantina. Standing at the bar talking to a local Mexican *patron* was Elena Mazour y Chavela, the Casa's owner.

His heart doubled its pace until he felt like some grammar school boy stealing glances at his sweetheart across the classroom. Sands studied the regal woman responsible for the race of his pulse. A cantina owner she might be, forced to earn a living after her father and brothers were killed fighting against Generalissimo Santa Anna for Texas independence, but Sands could not look at the woman without conjuring visions of European princesses and queens.

Dressed in a gown of royal blue with a lace shawl about her shoulders and lace fan in hand, no man would ever mistake her for anything but the lady she was. A lady whose head turned and jet-black eyes sparkled in greeting as they alighted on Sands. Inclining her head toward a vacant table, Elena's attention returned to the man beside her.

Although Sands could not hear her words, he knew that she hastily but politely concluded the conversation, a fact that proved true when she stepped to his side before he had half reached the empty table. Repressing the urge to take her in his arms and cover her mouth with his own, Sands simply grinned and nodded. After all, he had to protect the reputation of one of San Antonio's most beautiful ladies.

"For such a handsome man, Joshua Sands, you look like some desperate *bandido*!" She bit a full red lower lip as she studied him. "However, as soon as I heard you had returned with Captain Hays's company, I had Manuel draw a hot bath for you and lay out soap and a razor!''

The focus of those bright eyes was on the forest of hair bushed over Sands's cheeks, chin, and throat. He smiled. "You mean I've got to shave it off? It's just got to where I'm not scratching at it every five minutes.''

"Off! One should not hide such a handsome face, *mi corazon*. And those clothes go too! Your own have been cleaned and are hanging in my closet.'' The tone of her voice as well as her words left no doubt she would not argue about the beard.

"I had no intention of keeping this.'' Sands ran a hand over the thick growth of facial hair.

Actually, he had considered leaving the beard for a while. However, it would be easier facing a razor than butting heads with Elena. The angelic, sculptured Spanish beauty of her face, the diminutive size of the woman's shapely body were deceptive. Beneath that exquisite exterior was a passionate soul and a temper that could burn white hot in the batting of an eye. Sands had been on the wrong end of Elena's anger enough to know defying her was a losing proposition. The beard would go—and his Comanchero duds.

"That is good.'' She smiled coyly. "After all, I was not trained as a barber. I might have cut your throat had I been forced to shave you myself.''

Sands chuckled, again wanting to sweep this desirable bundle of alluring woman into his arms. "In fact,'' he assured her, "I'll shave the beard off this very instant.'' His gaze suggestively moved to the arched hallway to the left of the cantina's bar, the passageway that led to Elena's rooms.

"Not now, and not that way. I have too many patrons here, and they all have big eyes and ears," she answered. "Sit, and I will send Manuel over with a tequila. Have a drink, then leave. The back door has been left unlocked for you."

With a grin and a shrug of acceptance, Sands watched Elena return to the Casa de Chavela's patrons while he took a chair at the empty table.

A few moments later, Manuel, the cantina's bartender, brought a tray holding a double tequila with salt and lime. As he placed the drink before Sands, he whispered, "There will be a steak dinner waiting in the *señorita*'s chambers in fifteen minutes."

Thanking the small heavyset Mexican, Sands settled back in the chair and nursed the tequila for five minutes before pushing from the table and leaving the cantina. Outside, he remounted the bay, rode a couple of blocks south, then reined into an alley at the back of the Casa de Chavela, where he dismounted again.

Elena Chavela's chambers totaled five rooms, with the back door opening on to her bedroom. With a glance at the big four-poster bed positioned to the left side of this most intimate of rooms, Sands crossed to a door that led into the parlor. His objective was another doorway on the opposite side of the sitting room—a portal hung with strings of beads.

Pushing the strands aside, he entered the room and grinned. True to Elena's words, a huge wooden tub stood waiting for him. Misty fingers of steam rose in swirling columns from the water's surface. On the far side of the tub, beneath a mirror hung on the wall, was a small table. A filled washbasin, a shaving mug, leather strap, and open razor waited there.

Sands seated himself on the room's only chair, tugged off round-toed boots scuffed with the scratches and scars of hard use, stood to pull his shirt over his head and then skin down his breeches.

He grimaced as he slipped into the tub. If he had been a lobster, he'd have been screaming and his shell would have turned a bright red—the water was that hot! Yet by the time he sank neck deep in the bath, he sighed as the long miles on horseback eased from his muscles. The fist-sized bar of yellow lye soap he found on the floor beside the tub did wonders to remove the sands of Texas he carried in his hair and beard, not to mention the sweat and grime accumulated during his week on the trail.

"*Señor* Sands?" Manuel called to him.

"In here, my friend," Sands answered as he lounged back in the tub.

In his right hand, the bartender carried a tray containing a plate heaped with a thick mesquite-broiled beefsteak and boiled new potatoes, a mug, and a small coffeepot. In his left was a rough-hewn pine board. Manuel placed the board across the tub and set the tray atop it.

For a moment Sands considered asking the man if he often served his employer meals while she soaked in perfumed bathwater, then decided against it. What existed between Elena and Sands was something special. The time they had when they were together belonged to *them*. But when they were apart— Their silent agreement was that there were no questions asked.

"The *señorita* said that I was to remind you she placed a razor for you on that table," Manuel said as he exited the room to return to the cantina.

"I've seen it!" Sands called after the bartender. He then

sat straight in the water, found the knife and fork placed beside the plate, and attacked the meal as though he had been without food for a lifetime.

When he came up for air, the plate was clean and half the coffee was gone from the pot. Satisfied and full, he slowly extracted himself from the tub and dried with a towel hung over the back of the chair, then turned to the small table and the razor.

Slicing through the bramble of hair on his face was neither as relaxing as the bath nor as satisfying as the beefsteak. He grumbled, cussed, and winced as he managed to gingerly remove the thick growth from cheeks grown tender after a long time away from a blade.

The task was finally completed with only one small nick to his neck and a single small drop of blood. Feeling like a new man, Sands walked into the parlor and stepped to the mahogany mantel above the fireplace. He opened a cigar box that once belonged to Elena's father and selected a Cuban cigar from within. Lighting it with a thin splinter of kindling that he stuck into the low-burning fire in the hearth, he drew the blue smoke deep into his lungs and slowly exhaled it in a thin stream.

If Elena entertained other men in her chambers during his frequent and often long absences, he was unable to gauge those visits by the cigar box. Its contents appeared untouched since he last visited her rooms.

Drawing another puff from the cigar, Sands closed the box and shook his head as he walked into Elena's bedroom. What Elena did in his absence was of no concern to him, he told himself. And almost believed it.

Sands deposited the cigar in an ashtray on a night table beside the comforter-covered bed, then stretched out on the soft feather mattress. Locking his hands behind his head, he closed his eyes. Despite the convenient arrangement he shared with Elena, it was damned difficult not to wonder if others found comfort in the dark-tressed beauty's arms, tasted the sweetness of her lips, drank the warmth of her body.

"Joshua Sands!" Elena's voice, touched with irritation, wedged into Sands's mind. "I'm delighted that the prospect of my company is so exciting to you!"

Sands's eyes blinked open sleepily, and he smiled sheepishly up at the temptress who stood at the foot of the bed with hands planted firmly on her flaring hips. He had closed his eyes and drifted into sleep without knowing it.

"The ride today was long," he said, making no mention of Forty Horses and his braves. "Guess I was more tired than I thought."

"And I believed you when you said that I fired your blood like fine wine." The disappointment in her voice and the slight pout of her lower lip were teasing. She pulled the tortoiseshell combs from her hair to let the raven tresses seductively spill down about her shoulders in a rich, sleek cascade.

"The finest of wines," Sands assured her as he sat up and opened his arms in invitation.

A trace of a coy, flirting smile uplifted the corners of her ruby-red lips, and she shook her head in answer to his invitation. "A man's fingers are too clumsy for delicate hooks and buttons."

Her smile grew and she batted long dark eyelashes. "Besides, I like the feel of your eyes on me."

Those blue-gray eyes gave her their full attention as her arms languidly stretched behind her back and unfastened the hooks of her gown, then drew the lacy dress above her head and carefully deposited it over the back of a chair. Anticipation blazed in his gaze as Elena gracefully shed the layers of petticoat and cumbersome undergarments.

Then she stood before him, unashamed of her nakedness. Her nut-brown nipples poked into the air, firm and erect, as his loving gazes caressed the voluptuous mounds of her breasts. A delicious shiver of desire suffused him while his eyes stroked the flatness of stomach, the long, sensuous curve of her calves, the supple, shapely thighs, and that dark triangle of down below the deep well of her navel.

For an instant her own gaze dipped. Again a smile played at the corners of her mouth at the discovery that she had the total attention of more than just his eyes. Then she came to him all abounce and jiggling, surrendering herself to his mouth, his hands, and the urgent hunger of his young, lean, muscular body.

"Will Brown left for LaGrange today," Elena said as she lay atop Sands with her head on his chest. The soft stream of her breath trickled through the hairs of his chest. "He heard that a Captain Nicholas Dawson needed rangers there."

Sands's palms slowly stroked down the satin luxury of Elena's back to playfully knead the firm globes of her buttocks. Will Brown, the youngest ranger in Jack Hays's company, was a close friend. Although the younger man was a bit headstrong and reckless on occasion, Sands couldn't ask for a better man at his side. And like Sands, he had worked as a bouncer at the Casa de Chavela since Hays had released the majority of his company.

"I was afraid he'd do something like that," Sands answered. "He was getting restless."

"He waited for you to return for two days," Elena continued. "He was afraid to wait longer and miss the opportunity in LaGrange."

Sands nodded. In all likelihood, he would have ridden with Will had he been in San Antonio.

"And you, Joshua, are you getting restless?" Elena's head lifted, and she stared into Sands's eyes. "All the town knows that Captain Hays is looking for men to ride with him to Laredo. Has he approached you?"

"We talked about it." Sands's arms encircled her waist, drawing her close to revel in the womanly feel of her body.

"And?" A thinly puckered eyebrow arched above Elena's right eye.

"And . . . I'm thinking it over," he replied with a shrug.

The eyebrow drooped. "You'll go with him."

"I said that I was thinking it over." Sands lifted her delicate chin with a fingertip.

"And I said that you will go," she answered. "I am not a fool, Joshua Sands. You will ride with Captain Hays. He is your friend. When does the captain leave?"

"Tomorrow at noon," Sands said. "But at the moment, I haven't made up my mind. Laredo's a long way to the south and I just got back from—"

Elena's mouth and taunting tongue abruptly cut off his sentence. She wiggled a bit until she lay completely atop his outstretched body.

"You will go. That means we must make this night last until you come back to me," Elena said when their lips parted.

Sands didn't argue with her, in spite of the fact that he had not made up his mind. Instead, he once more turned his full attention to this desirable bundle of woman who so freely offered herself to him.

The next morning Sands quietly slipped from Elena's bed and dressed without disturbing the gentle rhythm of her breathing as she slept. Atop her armoire, he left the leather pouch Jess Qayle had given him. Elena would see that it was carefully tucked away with the rest of his savings.

Then he carefully opened the back door and stepped outside where his mount waited. There wasn't much time, but enough to gather supplies and gear by Jack Hays's noon deadline.

☆ SIX ☆

The clack of stones.

Josh Sands blinked, drawn up from warm dreams of Elena's satiny body and hungry embrace. Sleepily, his eyes fluttered closed again as he willed himself back into those caressing arms.

The snap of a dry twig.

The taunting brush of Elena's lips against his ear dissipated as did her alluring dream image. The young ranger brushed aside the cotton clogging his brain.

The whisper of a footstep in grass.

Not my imagination! Sands remained motionless, imitating sleep as he listened for the sound that had awakened him.

It came again. Closer now.

Not a boot. He forced his drowsy mind to swim through the molasses surrounding it. The sound lacked the harshness of a hard sole, even a boot carefully placed on the ground. It was no more than a—

Moccasin! Realization knifed through the last vestiges of sleep. He came fully alert. The whisper was that of a soft-skinned moccasin on the grass.

Sands's eyes opened to mere slits. There above him,

51

hovering like a giant shadow in the night's darkness, stood the source of those footsteps. Gaze creeping upward, the ranger's temples pounded. Revealed in the moon's silver light was a savage face painted in red and black—the colors of war to the *Nermernuh*!

High above that grisly visage rose the long shaft of a war lance. Moonlight ran along a flint spearhead aimed at the center of Sands's chest.

"*Comanche!*" A single word tore from the ranger's chest and throat as he cried out to warn the camp.

In the next instant, he rolled, body still wrapped in the confining blankets of his bedroll. The air was filled with a whistling swish that ended in a solid thud as the spearhead buried itself in the sandy soil.

Sands acted rather than thought. He threw the full weight of his blanket-entangled body into the lance's haft. The oak shaft jerked from the Comanche's hands and fell uselessly to the ground.

Surprise and disbelief washed over that war-painted face. One instant the brave had held death in his grip; in the next heartbeat, his hands lay empty!

In that brief moment of uncertainty, Sands managed to wiggle his left arm free of the confining blankets while his right hand burrowed at his side, seeking his still-holstered Colt. He couldn't find it!

"Aaaiiieeee!" A cry of frustration and rage ripped from the Comanche's lips.

The brave's hand dropped and wrenched a hunting knife free from a sheath that dangled at his waist. That spine-chilling cry once more tearing from his mouth, the warrior launched himself at the blanket-trapped ranger.

Again Sands's reaction came without conscious thought.

His left arm snaked upward, hand closing about the
Comanche's right wrist and jerking outward to redirect the
course of the descending blade.

That was enough to save him from the deadly sliver of
steel, but not from the brave himself. Sands groaned, air
forced from his lungs as the warrior's full weight slammed
atop him.

Before he could draw a steadying breath, the Comanche's
left hand covered his face, fingers groping, probing for his
vulnerable eyes. Sands jerked and twisted his head from
side to side in a desperate attempt to escape those gouging
fingers. Like the fangs of some feral animal, Sands's jaws
snapped open and closed as he strove to sink his teeth into
the brave's hand.

From somewhere in the distance, Sands heard the bark
of firing guns, bringing the camp alive. But of more
importance to him was the leather-wrapped handle his
right hand closed around—his own hunting knife!

While he struggled to keep the warrior's right arm pinned
beside him and avoid the fingers that sought his eyes, the
ranger tugged the blade from its scabbard and managed to
shift the honed tip upward. Then with all the strength he
could muster, he thrust.

There was a rent of fabric as the blade cut and tore
through the blankets. Then Sands felt an instant of resis-
tance just before the knife slid hilt deep into the Comanche's
stomach.

The warrior screamed, cold steel driven into his half-
naked body. He jerked upright, straddling Sands, his own
blade forgotten as agony seared through his gut.

Sands jerked the hunting knife free and thrust again, and
again. When he wrenched his blade from the Comanche's

abdomen for the fifth time, the brave crumpled to the side and lay still on the ground.

Kicking free of the encumbering bedroll, Sands stood in a wide-legged stance above the fallen Comanche, blade ready to strike again. There was no need. The last breath of life had passed from the warrior's body; he was dead.

Head spinning and heart pounding with the realization of how close death had brushed him this night, Sands sank slowly to the ground. He heard the scuff of booted feet around him.

"Josh, you all right?" The questioning voice belonged to Jack Hays.

Sands glanced up and nodded, unable to find his own voice as waves of nausea washed through him.

"All our men are safe and accounted for," Bill Simpson said from behind Sands. "Damned lucky, if you ask me. I thought Capt'n Perez had guards posted?"

"I did."

Sands turned to see Perez approach. The man was no taller than Hays and built just as wiry.

"Two of my men were standing guard," Perez said as he walked to Jack's side. "They're both dead now. Each took three arrows in the back. They never knew what hit them."

Jack sucked at his teeth and shook his head. "If it wasn't for Josh's warning, all our hair would be hanging from lodge poles." Hays tilted his head toward the warrior Sands had killed. "This one and four over there make five my men took."

"There's another six bodies back there," Perez replied with a glance to his men. "We were . . ."

Perez' words trailed off as one of his men walked to his side and whispered in his ear.

When Perez turned to Hays again, it was with a request. "Captain, this is Carlos Martin. His younger brother, Juan, was one of the two guards killed. He informs me there is a mission to the south near the hacienda of Antonio Navarro. He wishes to take his brother there for a proper burial . . . with your permission."

Sands glanced up at Hays as the ranger captain rubbed his chin. "Both men will get a decent burial. We'll ride for the Navarro ranch at sunup."

Hays paused for a moment, then looked back at Perez. "Until then I think we'd better triple the guard. These bucks might have friends lurking about."

As Perez returned to his men, Sands stood and asked Jack, "If you don't mind, I think I'll take a watch. Don't think I'll be able to get much sleep the rest of the night."

Jack nodded his approval and ordered four of his men to help dispose of the Comanche bodies. Sands wiped his knife clean and resheathed the blade. He glanced down at his Colt and shook his head. This night would be the last he slept with it holstered while on patrol. Henceforth the pistol would lay by his saddle within easy reach.

Licking the grease and the spicy sauce from his fingers, Sands returned the smile of an equally spicy young *señorita* who brushed past him with a jar of sweet wine in her arms. Batting long dark eyelashes, she gave her hips an exaggerated swing as she turned to serve the men.

"I don't understand it, Josh." Jack Hays sat at Sands's side, shaking his head. "You can't sit and eat dinner without drawing a lady's eye! Don't see what the women-folk see in a long, lanky, ill-mannered lout like you!''

Sands chuckled and lifted another piece of *cabrito* from the wooden tray resting on the ground before him. Jack was one to talk. Half the ladies in San Antonio went into a swoon when he entered the room. "I seen more than one feminine gaze giving you the once over.''

Sands sunk his teeth into the tender barbecued kid as his captain lifted his eyebrows and smiled.

"Noticed that myself. And if it weren't for Garcia, I'd be sorely tempted.''

"Garcia?'' Sands's gaze roved over the scene before him as he washed the *cabrito* down with a healthy swallow of wine. Antonio Navarro had opened his hacienda to the company, providing a minor feast of goat, *frijoles,* and tortillas for the men who camped on his land, not to mention a hogshead of wine and several eye-catching serving girls. "Is that one of Captain Perez' men?''

Jack licked his fingers. "A Mexican captain who's got troops outside Laredo. Navarro told Perez and me about him after the funerals this afternoon. Our host was down Laredo way about a week back. Seems Agaton and this Garcia are friends.''

Sands grimaced. "Which means we've got to ride into Laredo fast, snatch up Agaton, and ride the hell out before Captain Garcia realizes what's happening.''

"That's the way I would ordinarily handle it.'' Jack tossed a clean-picked rib bone into the night behind them. "Trouble is, Navarro says word of our coming has preceded us. Garcia is patrolling north of the border with his men, just waiting for us to show our faces.''

Drawing a deep breath, Sands released it in a long

disapproving whistle. The only advantage a small company of men had was surprise. Now they had lost that. "Seems like it's going to be hell earning that ten dollars you promised me."

Jack smiled without a trace of humor. "It does look rather bleak."

Rather bleak. Sands groaned inwardly. Jack had a bad habit of understating the situation. The prospect of riding into a town as hostile as Laredo was bleak. The possibility of facing trained Mexican soldiers with so small a company of men was insanity.

"Know anything about this Captain Garcia?" Sands probed with the hope Jack had an ace hidden up his sleeve.

"Just another Mexican officer who's fled north because his political party is out of favor in Mexico City," Jack replied. "Navarro couldn't even give me an estimate on the number of men with him."

Downing the remainder of the wine in the small pottery jug he used for a glass, Sands did his best to push down the fingers of dread that were climbing his back. "And you still intend to ride right into Laredo and take Agaton?"

Jack sat silent for several long moments, as though his mind was elsewhere, then his head moved slowly from side to side. "Don't know? Got any ideas?"

It was Sands's turn to sit silently, then shake his head.

"Hell of a lot of help you are." Jack sucked at his teeth in disgust.

"What'd ya expect from a ten-dollar ranger?" Sands answered while he placed his empty plate on the ground, stood, and stretched. "I'm just a long, lanky lout, remember? And you're the captain. They pay you to pull rabbits out of a hat like some medicine-show magician."

"Well, at the moment my hat doesn't have anything but one worried head in it." Jack glanced up to notice Sands starting toward a barn to their left. "Hey, where you going?"

"Noticed a nice fresh stack of straw in that barn earlier," Sands said, glancing back over a shoulder. "Thought it would make a nice bed for the night."

"Mean you're going to . . ." Hays's words fell away.

Also walking toward the large barn was the young *señorita* who had eyed Sands earlier. Hays smiled as he watched his friend follow the obviously willing woman into the barn's dark interior. After all, Sands had not mentioned sleeping, only finding a bed for the night.

☆ SEVEN ☆

Sands's gaze scanned the desolate terrain stretching end-lessly before him. The scenery varied little from the low humpbacked bluff on which the ranger had halted the bay. A harvest of rocks, sand, prickly pear, peyote cactus, and more rocks lay about him for as far as the eye could see.

Sands shook his head in disbelief. He considered the hill country about San Antonio to be a rugged, harsh land. This was a piece of Hell itself—south Texas!

Near the horizon a dark ribbon ran through the sandy browns of the desert. That ribbon was the narrow stream that bore the name the Rio Grande River whose waters ran shallow enough for a man to ford on foot ninety-eight percent of the time. Across the Rio Grande lay the state of Tamaulipas, Mexico.

Sands's attention focused neither on the Rio Grande nor on Laredo—a clump of low-slung adobe buildings that sat on the river's bank. Instead, he squinted at a wispy feather of white alkaline dust that swirled in the air halfway between his position and the town.

Spitting a dark stream of tobacco juice to the ground, the ranger shoved a wad of tobacco into his cheek with his tongue, then dug a hand into the bedroll tied behind his saddle. The hand pulled free, grasping a three-sectioned brass telescope. Sands extended the spyglass to its full length and lifted it to his eye.

His eye grew wide, then narrow as he located the wind-raked dust cloud. The source of that wispy white feather was a troop of mounted Mexican soldiers riding in double file.

"Sonofabitch." Sands did a hasty head count of the file of north-moving troop.

Eighteen rifle-and-saber-bearing men in each of the two long lines. Plus an officer in a plumed hat who rode point. That was thirty-seven in all. And they were only five miles away.

Lowering the telescope, Sands crammed the three sections together with a palm and shoved the instrument back into his sleeping roll. There were now only twenty-five men in Hays's company.

Wheeling the bay's head with a tug on the braided reins, the ranger dug his spurs into the horse's flanks, driving the gelding back downhill in a full run toward Jack and the other men who followed a mile behind.

Sands's anger-narrowed eyes shifted down the line of twenty kneeling men to John Coffee Hays. In disgust he spat the remnants of his tobacco chaw to the ground.

He felt like a target in a Thanksgiving turkey shoot, kneeling here in the middle of open desert without rock or scrub oak for protection. The participants in that target practice now approached—Captain Garcia and his thirty-six men, still mounted and with rifles ready.

Sands tried to ignore the beads of sweat that prickled

over his forehead. All the Mexican officer had to do was
order a charge and it would be over. If the ranger company
made a mad scramble for the horses behind them, they
would be cut down by sabers—if not by lead first.

How can Jack be such a stupid bastard? In spite of the
fact that he knelt with one knee in the sand and rifle
raised to greet Garcia's troop, Sands still couldn't believe
Hays had ordered the company to make a stand in such
rigid military formation, especially when the Mexican soldiers out-numbered the company.

Sands swiped at his brow with the sleeve of his shirt and
muttered a curse describing Jack's parental relationship to
a mongrel dog. This was total insanity. Hays should have
taken them Comanche style, ambushing the soldiers as
they rode between two of the low rolling hills. At least that
would have whittled down their numbers and evened up
the odds. Then the company could have taken the rest with
their Colts.

That's the way Sands saw it, and so he had told Hays.

"Josh, you don't understand the military mind," Jack
had replied. "Garcia will never order a charge. Mexican
officers are too enamored with the European style of
soldiering. He'll dismount his men and face us head-on. If
we can lick him on his own terms, he'll know he's been
beaten. Take him like we would a band of Comanche and
we'll give him a hundred excuses for his defeat—enough
for him to rouse all of Laredo against us. Defeating Garcia
isn't enough. We've got to do it on his own terms."

Captain Perez had nodded his agreement. "We've got to
make Garcia believe he's facing a small but well-trained
troop of Texian soldiers, not a band of marauding *bandidos*.
Besides, my men do not have Colts."

"We'll do this my way, Josh," Hays had concluded, ordering the men to dismount.

While three of Perez' men had gathered the reins and led the horses out of the line of fire, the rest of the company had taken their places in neat and vulnerable military formation.

So it was that Sands swung from his horse, primed his rifle, and knelt to wait beneath the Texas sun as Captain Garcia and his troop rode to meet the ranger patrol that had come for the outlaw Agaton.

Captain Garcia halted his soldiers a hundred yards from the Texian line of defense. The officer ordered his men to dismount, then edged his horse forward another twenty yards.

"Captain Hays and Captain Perez," Garcia called out in perfect English. "I have awaited your arrival for days. Your journey has been long and tiring, while my men and myself are fresh and rested. Throw down your weapons and surrender or be overwhelmed by my superior forces!"

In equally perfect Spanish, Jack Hays's normally quiet voice boomed out to his men, "Ready your weapons."

Sands and the rest of the company answered with a chorus of cocking hammers.

"So be it!" Garcia reined his gray mount about, then called over his shoulder. "No quarter will be given!"

Sands sighted down the barrel of his long rifle. He watched the Mexican captain return to his troops, who now stood with rifles ready. Behind them, five of their number held their mounts at bay. Garcia raised an arm and one of the men guarding the horses lifted a bugle.

"Hold your fire until my signal!" Jack called above the blaring call to attack. "Let them get—"

Jack's words were drowned by a roaring cry that went up from Garcia's soldiers. They charged! Rifles held at waist level with muzzles aimed at the Texian line, they ran forward in precise infantry formation.

Ninety yards, Sands estimated the distance between him and the attacking Mexicans. Despite his deep-seated feeling that Hays had misjudged the way of handling Garcia, he did admit Jack had called the shots correctly so far. *Seventy yards*.

When charging soldiers had traversed half the distance from the ranger company, Jack raised his own rifle and fired.

Immediately twenty Texian rifles answered the barking report of their captain's rifle. And just as quickly, Sands's view was obscured by dark smoke, the vicious, momentarily blinding cloud left by exploding black powder.

"Hit the ground!" Jack's voice cried out.

Sands didn't question the order but threw himself forward into the desert sands. Beyond the clearing haze of smoke came the crack of Mexican rifles. Sands glanced up and did a double take.

Garcia's men no longer charged, but had turned and now ran back toward their waiting horses. One man lay dead on the ground, only one, and he wore a Mexican uniform.

Sands sucked at his teeth. He had hoped half of Garcia's troop would lay strewn in the sand, cut down by the rangers' volley. Such was the unreliability of black-powder loads. While he had seen men pick off squirrels from the top branches of a tree at a hundred yards away with long rifles, he had also seen the same rifles fired point-blank at a target and miss.

"Reload!" Hays called.

Sands scrambled to his knees and yanked the ramrod from beneath the barrel of his rifle. In went fresh powder, cotton wad, and lead ball, and he lifted the rifle, ready for another charge. There was none. The Mexicans, with Garcia at their head, sat astride their mounts once again, riding in retreat.

"Injuries?" Hays called out for a casualty report.

He waited but no answer came. Sands glanced around, and his gaze confirmed the silence—none of his companions had sustained an injury.

"Then what the hell are you waiting for? Mount up, men!" Jack ordered and waved for the horses to be brought forward.

"Damn, Capt'n, they turned tail without much of a fight!" This from Bill Simpson, Hays's second-in-command. "Can't believe we licked 'em so easily!"

"It ain't over." Jack swung into the saddle. "Garcia will be waiting for us down the road apiece." Jack's gaze went out over his company, making certain all were mounted, then signaled them forward.

Sands grimaced as he reined his bay beside the ranger captain. Garcia's charge had only been to test his opponent's strength. The Mexican officer had expected the ranger company to break rank and flee. When the adversaries met again, Garcia would be ready for a fight.

That meeting came a mile closer to Laredo. Once again the Mexican officer had dismounted his troops and lined them across the road. Bayonets now glinted from rifles

leveled for a charge. Captain Garcia and two fellow officers remained mounted behind the line.

Sands turned to Jack and smiled. The brazen boldness of
the first attack was gone. In that he retained his mount,
Garcia now was conceding the possibility of defeat at the
hands of the Texians. Like their European counterparts
Mexican officers fled the battlefield rather than face surrender with their troops.

"Same position as before!" Jack signaled his men from
their horses. "Hold your fire until my command!"

Leather creaked as the troops with rifles in hand stepped
from their saddles once more, ready to kneel in a defensive
line before the Mexican troops. Sands's left foot had not
cleared the stirrup when a yowling cry went up from
Garcia's men. His head jerked around and he cursed.

The Mexicans were charging!

"Get the horses out of the line of fire!" Jack called to
the men who had been given charge of the mounts. Then,
to the rest of the company, "Hold your fire until my
signal!"

Someone yanked the bay's reins from Sands's hands.
The young ranger pivoted and hefted his rifle. At the same
instant, the line of advancing soldiers fired. Man-made
thunder rolled across the south Texas desert.

A pained groan came from Sands's right. Out of the
corner of his eye, he saw Will Simpson clutch at a moist
crimson flower that blossomed on his upper left arm. With
gritted teeth, Jack's second-in-command jerked his rifle to
his right shoulder and turned to face the charging line of
blue-and-white-uniformed Mexicans.

"Form your rank!" This from Jack. "They're out of
lead now, boys!"

They still got those damned pig-stickers on the end of their rifles! Sands cursed silently as he took his place in the defensive line. He started to kneel as before. His knee never touched the sand.

"Charge!" Hays's voice railed. "Burn 'em with powder!"

The company's formation might have imitated a well-trained military troop, but the bloodcurdling cries that tore from the men's throats were those learned from the lords of the plains—the Comanches! In a tight line the rangers charged, ready to meet the uniformed death that barreled down at them.

Again Sands mentally judged the distance between him and Garcia's forces. At forty yards came Hays's command to fire. Without thought, Sands squeezed down on his trigger. The sound of his own report was lost in the deafening roar of twenty-two rifles firing in unison.

And still they charged, pushing through the haze of gunsmoke to find Garcia's soldiers running in a mad scramble toward their waiting mounts.

"Halt!" Jack's command rose over the rangers' battle cry. "Reload!"

Before Sands stumbled to a halt, Garcia and his men remounted and reined their horses toward Laredo. Quickly reloading his rifle, Sands turned to Jack. "This could go on all day!"

"Injuries?" Jack called out, ignoring his friend's comment.

Again there was no answer although Sands could see Simpson and two of Perez' men clutching at bloody wounds in their thighs. Jack saw the same thing and ordered the wounded men to take the place of those assigned to handling the mounts.

After Jack gave the order to climb back in the saddle, he looked at Sands. "I'm not going to let this take all day. I want to break Garcia before he can get to Laredo and reinforcements."

The ranger captain then signaled his men to approach him. "Boys, this is the way we're going to handle it . . ."

☆ EIGHT ☆

Captain Garcia and his troop awaited the ranger company two miles to the south. While the Mexican army captain and two of his fellow officers sat on horseback, their troops formed that now-familiar line. The soldiers, however, did not stand ready for another charge, but knelt in the sand with rifles raised and ready.

Sands's head jerked around and he flashed Jack a broad grin. The ranger captain had once again predicted Garcia's action—a defensive stand rather than an offensive charge. Following his quickly laid plan, Hays halted his company two hundred yards from the Mexican line.

"Dismount and take your positions, men," Jack ordered and waited until the company stood on the ground before dismounting himself.

As he had done twice before, the young captain completely abandoned ranging strategy. His answer to Garcia's defensive line was a simple European military tactic. Instead of a single offensive line, the company formed two ten-man ranks, the second directly behind the first.

"You boys know what's expected of you." Jack's voice was low, deadly low, as he surveyed the enemy ahead. "And that's all I want from you . . . no more, no less."

Sands, who stood at Hays's side in the first line of attack, realized that soft tone carried unspoken meaning. Hays would shoot the first man who broke rank and fled. But then there was no need for a verbal threat. Every man in the company knew Jack Hays and his ways.

"Okay, boys, let's have at 'em—slow and steady." Hays's right arm rose, then fell forward.

At the drop of his friend's arm, Sands stepped forward. The nine men beside him did likewise. Without a sound, except for the steady crunch of sand and rock beneath boots, they moved toward the line of Mexican rifles whose unbobbing muzzles were raised to meet their attack.

Ten paces covered and Sands heard Perez give the order for the second rank to move forward.

"Slow and easy, men," Jack whispered to his company. "They ain't nothing but flesh and blood."

So it was, rifle at waist level and face set in cool determination, that Sands crossed twenty yards, fifty, a hundred. Only when fifty yards separated them from the unmoving line of soldiers did Jack's arm jerk into the air again.

Sands halted, as did the men beside him. Rifles went from waist to shoulders, eyes sighting down long barrels of gray steel.

"Fire!" Hays's arm fell.

Ten rifles cracked in a single booming voice. Smoke billowed, and the acrid smell of gunpowder filled the air.

"Reload!" Hays's voice cut through the echoing rifle report.

Without question, Sands and the rest of the front line dropped to one knee and grasped their powder horns.

Mexican rifles barked! Stone whined in ricochet as hot

lead slapped into the ground at Sands's right foot. A brand of fire laced upward along the ranger's right calf.

"Sonofabitch!" Sands grasped at his leg, feeling a sticky warmth trickle onto fingers and palm. With another curse he lifted his hand.

"Bad?" Jack stared down at him, brow furrowed.

"Creased the skin," Sands answered, sucking in a steadying breath through his teeth to fight back the burning pain of the wound.

"Drown it in bourbon later. Right now get that rifle loaded!" Jack's gaze moved down the offensive line, checking the condition of his men. Approval lifted the corners of his mouth when he found no other injuries.

By the time Sands ramrodded cotton wad and ball into the muzzle of his weapon, Perez and the second line passed by their kneeling companions and became the front line of offense. Calmly, steadily they marched toward the reloading Mexicans.

"On your feet, men," Jack called out.

The line had no more than regained their feet when Perez's men opened fire. Immediately they knelt to reload and allow Hays's line to take the offensive. The haze of gunsmoke cleared. Three Mexican soldiers lay facedown in the sand—three rifles fewer to provide an answering volley from Garcia's line.

While Perez's men reloaded, Hays's rank emptied fresh loads into the line of blue-and-white uniforms. Two more soldiers dropped before Garcia ordered his men to fire once again.

Beside him, Sands heard an agonizing groan. He didn't have time to glance around. Jack shouted for the line to reload their long rifles. Dropping to a knee, Sands did just that, while Perez's men once again marched to the lead and spat lead into the Mexican defensive.

At Hays's command, Sands and the line rose, strode forward, took aim, fired, and dropped to reload as Perez and his men marched past. Sands's head jerked up—something was wrong, different. There was no answering volley from the soldiers.

Wrong, hell! Sands's grin split his face. Nothing was wrong—everything was right!

Garcia's soldiers hadn't answered that last round because they no longer held their weapons. The Mexicans' rifles lay in the sand at their feet and their arms were raised high above their heads in surrender. Even the five men assigned to the soldiers' horses were shouting for mercy.

Behind the surrendering troop, Garcia and his two companions wheeled their mounts and spurred hell bent for leather back toward the Rio Grande and Laredo.

"They're in range, Captain," a man said from beside Sands. "Should we try and pick them off?"

Jack shook his head. "Garcia's just the messenger we need to announce our impending arrival in Laredo. Let him go."

Hays glanced to Perez and his men, who rushed to surround the survivors of Garcia's original thirty-six men. "Best give Antonio a hand, boys. And be sure none of those Mexican horses get away. You'll get more for them than the ten dollars the republic's paying for your services."

A cheer of victory went up from the men as they rushed forward to claim the spoils of today's battle. Both horses and Mexican rifles would supplement the low pay they would receive when they returned to San Antonio.

"What about the prisoners?" Sands asked as he glanced at his friend.

"We'll leave the dead and strip the rest," Jack answered with a grin. "Then we'll march 'em right down Laredo's main street."

Sands gritted his teeth and told the wizened old Mexican physician tending his calf wound just where his soul would spend eternity. The old man chuckled and poured another shot of tequila over the long red welt that ran up the ranger's calf before wrapping it in a white bandage.

"Quit your bellyachin', Josh. Ain't nothing but a scratch," Bill Simpson said with a laugh and a shake of his head. "You could have this."

Simpson proudly sported a sling that cradled his left arm.

"And you could be wearing this size eleven up your backside!" Sands grunted as he tugged his boot back on his foot.

Sands realized how lucky he and the rest of the company were. Six injuries in all, and Simpson's arm wound was the worst by far. The rest had been flesh wounds like the one he bore. Painful to be certain, but no man had ever died from having his hide creased a bit.

The same could not be said of Garcia's troop. Eight soldiers had been left facedown in the desert. Another ten were now nursing wounds or waiting for the doctor to dig lead from arms and legs.

Not to mention bruised feet, Sands thought as he slid off the physician's operating table. While Jack had stopped short of stripping the captives down to their bare nothings, he had ordered them to remove their boots for the eight-mile march into Laredo. Prisoners picking their way over rock and cactus have little time to concern themselves with attacking their captors.

"Capt'n Jack said for us to meet him as soon as we were doctored up," Simpson said, nodding to the door to the doctor's office.

"If you're waiting on me, you're wasting time," Sands answered as he followed the company's second-in-command outside with a slight limp. His leg was stiff and sore, but by the time the company returned to San Antonio, a thin white scar would be all that remained to remind him of today's battle.

Half a block down the wide band of dust and sand that served as Laredo's main street, Hays and Perez stood talking with the town's *alcalde* and three other of the town's representatives. The four men turned and quickly strode down the street as Simpson and Sands joined the two captains.

"Looks like we did the right thing letting Garcia and his two lieutenants go." Jack grinned broadly. "He hightailed right back here with word that Texas had sent an army to take over Laredo. Then he and his two men jumped the river back into Mexico."

"Taking half of Laredo's most prominent citizens with him," Perez added with a grin as wide as Hays's. "It seems Captain Garcia's report of our ferocity caused such consternation among Laredo's gentle citizens that they feared they too would become our captives."

"And Agaton?" Sands's eyes narrowed at the report that so many of Laredo's residents had fled back across the border into northern Mexico. "Did he jump the river too?"

"Thought so at first," Jack answered. "But after I assured the *alcalde* that we hadn't come to take his city from him—that all we wanted was to secure safety for Texian traders—Laredo's fair mayor admitted that Agaton is holed up drunk in a room behind that cantina."

Hays pointed to a shingle proclaiming food and tequila that hung in front of a building at the end of the street. "The *alcalde* has gone to retrieve Agaton for us at this very moment. With luck we should be on our way back to San Antonio by tomorrow morning."

"So grateful are Laredo's remaining citizens," Perez said, "that the *alcalde* has welcomed us into his town, praising us for ridding him of such *desperados*. He has ordered the women of the town to prepare a feast in our honor this night."

Jack and Perez laughed, as did Sands and Simpson. To be sure, Texian rangers might not be welcome here on the border, but that they came for so little and would be gone so quickly gave Laredo's citizens reason for celebration.

Garcia's defeat would also give other Mexican officers second thoughts before they brought troops across the Rio Grande and into Texas again. Sands glanced at Jack, unashamed of the admiration he felt for the man.

Hays had come for Agaton and had gotten him. At the same time, he had delivered a message to Mexico that although this portion of south Texas was difficult to patrol, it was still Texas and Texians would keep it.

Sands shook his head. Only this morning he had silently berated Jack for his stubborn insistence on facing Garcia's troops as a military unit rather than a ranging company.

Jack had been correct in his decision, and he had been wrong. But then that was why Hays was a captain, and he was merely a ranger.

Boots returned to their feet and heads hanging low, the survivors of Garcia's troop crossed the Rio Grande back into Mexico the next morning under the watchful eye of Captain John Coffee Hays and his ranger company. When the soldiers were no more than a dust cloud in the distance, Hays lifted an arm and signaled his men northward back to San Antonio.

With his bay's braided reins lightly held in his left hand, and his right tightly about a rope encircling the neck of a black mare at his side, Sands gladly complied with the order, moving beside Hays and Bill Simpson. The mare, sleek and spirited, was Sands's prize, picked from the captured Mexican horses. No mustang this, but a thoroughbred that would easily bring a hundred dollars at auction—if Sands decided to sell the mare.

"Doesn't look like much," Hays said as they rode northward.

"What? Jack, what the hell are you talking about? Most men would give their right arm to have a mare like this." Sands's head jerked around, his admiring eyes leaving the mare's sleek lines and homing in on the ranger captain.

Jack shook his head, then nodded back to Agaton, who rode at the center of the company, surrounded by four men. "Would have thought he was a bigger man from all I heard about him."

Sands admitted Agaton was shorter and stockier than he

expected. Even on horseback he looked small. "It's the chains. They make most men look small."

"Never was a big man," Hays said, sucking at his teeth. "Just had guns. Take them away from him and he's what he's always been—a little man."

☆ NINE ☆

Sands's gaze slowly roved over the Casa de Chavela. He grunted, a sound that echoed the disinterest held in his steel-blue eyes. Reaching for the tequila bottle at the center of the round table, he poured a shot of the golden liquor into a glass, lifted it, and tossed down the drink in one swallow.

Pour, lift, gulp! How many times had he repeated that same sequence of actions since he entered the cantina? How long had he been in the Casa?

He slipped his watch from a pocket and thumbed open its lid. The slightly blurred hands read 9 P.M. He had walked into the cantina at five that afternoon, he recalled. His mind stumbled awkwardly through a gentle haze of alcohol as he mentally ciphered the difference. *Four hours,* he decided with a glance back to the bottle, *and this bottle's still half full. Must be losing my touch.*

His gaze made another circuit around the cantina. Only five of the tables, including his own, were occupied. Elena's three girls sat at one of those tables, whispering and laughing among themselves. There was little else to do. The Casa de Chavela's patrons gave no notice to the shapely calves and ankles revealed by the daringly high cut of their dress hems. Wednesday was a slow business night, even in a frontier town like San Antonio.

Sands found no trace of the cantina's lovely proprietor. He shrugged, remembering as the undulating tequila mist parted for a moment.

Elena had been here . . . at this very table, he told himself with a confirming bob of his head. *Then she got all huffy and stomped off like there was a burr under her saddle.* Not that he blamed her for leaving. After all, he was the cause of her irritation and frustration.

When he strode into the Casa de Chavela that afternoon, he had but one purpose in mind—to drink himself into a drunken stupor, to stop the ceaseless churning of his mind. Elena had been there for him, a willing substitute for alcohol, an understanding ear to hear out his problems.

Understand? How could she understand? He gave another disgruntled snort, then shook his head in an admission that Elena did truly understand what was eating at his gut. *Understands me more than I like to admit!*

She had tried to cajole him away from the bottle. And when that didn't work, she had tried anger, fury, and curses. All of which had been equally unsuccessful.

"Men! Men and their dark moods! And you, Joshua Sands, are the worst! Like a child you sit there sulking and basking in self-pity." She had pushed from the table, firmly planted hands on hips, and glared down. "Tonight you can drown your self-pity in tequila. As for me, I'm going to bed and sleep. I'll waste no more time or words on you this night!"

She had stormed across the cantina and down that arched hall to her chambers, leaving him alone to nurse the tequila bottle. He had only shrugged in answer.

As he shrugged now. Elena had been right. It was self-pity gnawing at him. But dammit, he couldn't shake it—or the cause of that self-pity. He was on his own again—no longer a ranger! A week had passed since he had returned to San Antonio, and he was unable to free himself of the feeling that he was lost, adrift without roots to anchor him to life. Ranging had been all he had known since he had lost his family. It was his life. Now that life had been severed once again.

To be certain, Elena offered him employment in the cantina. He had done that once, but never again. He saw nothing wrong with being a bouncer—until something else came along. Nor did he mind a woman as an employer— any woman but Elena. What he and Elena shared had nothing to do with employee and employer, and he wanted to keep it that way. It was as simple as that.

And I'm not cut out for farming or clerking, he thought, with the realization that both occupations were far too staid for a man accustomed to patrolling the frontier. *Not that I've had any experience at doing either!* he also admitted. *Damned politicians! Ain't got the sense they were born with!*

Sands once again reached for the bottle's neck. It was easier to slide another shot down his throat than to ponder about things over which he had no control. If the Congress in Austin said the republic's treasury lacked the funds to maintain full ranging companies, there was nothing he could do about it. No way to fight the decisions of men who paid more attention to the merchants of the East then to the settlers who lived with the threat of Comanche attack both day and night.

And Mexican attack! Sands mentally added that ever-present danger facing the Republic of Texas. Mexico wanted her Texas territory returned to her; one day she would send an invasion force north to reclaim it.

Let the politicians stand up to the Mexican army! Sands grunted with displeasure as he hefted the bottle from the table. *Wonder how long they'd keep those fancy beaver hats on their heads under a volley of Mexican rifles!*

"Care to buy a man a drink?"

Sands's head shakily jerked up, and he stared into the ebony face of his former partner, Benjamin Franklin Webb. Ben's ivory-white smile, which appeared to run from one ear to another, faded as he peered down at Sands.

"You look like hell!" Ben waved for Manuel to bring another glass from the bar, then plopped down in a chair across the table from Sands. "Decided to take up residence in that bottle?"

"For tonight at least," Sands answered with a snort as Manuel brought the requested glass. The ranger then poured Ben a shot and filled his empty glass. He eyed the remaining tequila for a moment. "Care to join me? Looks like there'll be room enough for two soon as this is empty."

"Might as well. Not particular who I drink with." Ben nodded to his friend, lifted his glass, and drained it in one healthy swallow. "Damn, that's good! Beats eating dust— and words."

Sands lifted an eyebrow. "You been wandering around the Comanche camps again?"

Ben shook his head as he poured a second shot and downed it with the same relish as the first. "Been trying to make myself a legitimate landowner in the fair Republic of Texas."

Sands's eyebrow arched higher. "A farmer? You thinking of plowing the land?"

The former slave laughed as he helped himself to a third drink. "Horse breeder—a landed gentleman!"

"Horse breeder?" Sands puzzled, then remembered Ben's chestnut mare. "Louisville Lady?"

"Yep." Ben winked and lifted his glass again, but only sipped at the tequila this time. "One of these days that mare will be makin' my fortune—but not today."

Sands thought of his bay gelding and the black thoroughbred mare still stabled at the ranger garrison. Both were fine specimens of horseflesh, but neither would ever make him a fortune. "Neither you nor me are cut out to be rich men, my friend."

"You might not be," Ben replied, perusing his half-drunk friend over the lip of his glass, "but I damn sure intend to have a go at it! Today I would have been on my way if I'd—"

"Today?" Sands's tongue felt thick and unmanageable. "What's so special about today?"

"That's what I was trying to tell you." Ben shook his head and finished off his drink. "There's an old man outside town called Mylius who's selling off his farm. A thousand acres at a dollar an acre. I rode—"

"Sylvester Mylius?" Sands watched Ben nod. "I once did some business with Mylius. Rented a barn and bit of pasture from him for a couple of months for a friend of mine." Sands didn't mention that friend had been a woman who he had once hoped to marry. "Why is Mylius wanting to sell out?"

"A brother of his died and left him a passel of land up around Coffeeville ways," Ben replied. "Seems he'd rather grow cotton in east Texas than fight off the rattlers here in the hill country.''

"Did you strike a deal with him?" Sands asked.

"A fair deal—trouble is I'm four hundred short. Mylius wants cash on the barrelhead, flat out and straight down." Ben poured himself another shot of tequila. "And there ain't a man in the whole Republic of Texas that's going to give no nigger a loan."

Taking half the shot in a gulp, Ben grinned across the table at Sands. "You ain't happened to got four hundred in loose change lyin' around, do you?"

"Might." Sands shrugged. In fact he had six hundred socked away. "But I don't see how that mare of yours will ever make you rich. She's only one mare, and there aren't that many men in Texas rich enough to go the price you place on her."

"Ain't got no mind to go and sell Louisville Lady. Told you I was goin' into the horse-breeding business." Ben placed his glass on the table and stared at Sands, his face suddenly sober. "That mare's got bloodlines that run all the way back to the Garden of Eden. Crossbreed that, and a man'll have a horse every man in this country will be hankerin' to buy."

"Crossbreed? With what?" Sands snorted.

"A mustang," Ben said simply.

"A *mustang*?" Sands couldn't believe what he heard. Only the Comanches and Apaches had any use for the herds of wild horses that ran free on the plains.

"A mustang stud," Ben repeated, undaunted by his friend's skepticism. "He'll make a handsome husband for Louisville Lady. Of course, the opposite should be true, so

I've got a thoroughbred stallion stabled in Austin to handle all those fillies running free!''

"*You've* been running free too long—in the sun without a hat. Burned your brain to a crispy black cinder!'' Sands sucked at his teeth, still unable to accept what Ben proposed. "What man would want a cross between a thoroughbred and a mustang?''

"Just about any man in the republic, if you'd just open your mind and give it a think,'' Ben answered. "Dammit, Josh, think! Why does Capt'n Jack require his men to own a mount worth at least a hundred dollars?''

"Speed,'' Sands answered. "Got to have a horse that's fleet ahoof.''

"And what kind of horse can give you that speed?'' Ben pressed.

"A thoroughbred,'' Sands answered again.

Ben nodded and smiled. "That's right. It's something every man and boy in Texas knows—white or black. But it's the next part that will take some serious pondering.''

Sands nodded when his friend paused to make certain he had the ranger's attention. "Go on, I'm listening.''

Taking a deep breath, Ben asked, "How often have you ever outrun a Comanche war party?''

"Depends,'' Sands said with a shrug. "If the chase is no more than two miles, five at the most, we usually overtake them.''

"But if the ride's longer, those bucks will leave you eating their dust. Why?'' Ben's eyes narrowed.

"Horses tire out,'' Sands said.

"The Comanches' ponies don't tire out,'' Ben said with wisdom in his voice. "Mustangs might lack a thoroughbred's burst of speed, but they more than make up for it in endurance. Hell, you know as well as I do that a warrior can make a hundred miles in one night if he's got two mustangs to carry him. How far you reckon you could ride on the backs of two thoroughbreds in a night?''

Sands's brow furrowed. Was he crazy or was Ben making sense? Comanche ponies were known for their endurance. Even Jack Hays cursed the ruggedness of Indian mounts.

''Mustangs are a hearty breed, Josh. They've had to be. They're the great-great-great-grandchildren of horses that escaped from the first Spanish explorers who rode through this land. They've survived. The land molded them, made them tough and strong.''

Sands's brow knitted even deeper. He must be crazy, because Ben *was* making sense. Why hadn't anyone ever considered crossbreeding with mustangs before?

''Think about it, Josh.'' Ben leaned toward him. ''Mustangs are the horses of the plains. They can live off buffalo grass and mesquite beans if need be. You've got to oat and hay a thoroughbred regularly if it's going to survive in this country. Crossbreed and we can get the best from both animals.''

''I am thinking,'' Sands answered. The possibilities had his head aspin. Or was it the tequila? ''And you want me to loan you the money?''

''Or we could go in as partners,'' Ben said. ''That is, if you've got the four hundred.''

''I've got the four hundred—and a damned pretty little mare that I'd match against your Louisville Lady any day of . . .'' He caught himself. What Ben proposed was exciting, but what kind of partner would he make for Ben? ''Hell, Ben, I don't know beans from horse apples about running a breeding ranch.''

"Don't have to—I do. I learned it the hard way," Ben said, making it obvious the knowledge had come during the time he had been shackled with slave chains. "I won't need a hand to help me run the place, leastways not at first. What I do need is a grubstake. Throw in with me, and we'll go at it fifty-fifty. I'll do the work that needs doing."

"Fifty-fifty," Sands mused aloud, then stared up at his friend. "Don't you worry about me doing my fair share. I'm not afraid of a little work."

Ben's voice tightened as he obviously tried to contain his excitement. "Then you want to go in on Mylius' place?"

"Right now I've got enough tequila in me to want to go in on anything," Sands said, trying to keep a hold on his common sense. "I need time to think about it. Let my mind clear and look at this in the light of day."

"Fair enough," Ben said as he poured two fresh drinks. He then lifted his glass. "To our new partnership!"

Sands's own glass rose, and just before killing off the shot, he said, "Maybe."

☆ TEN ☆

Sands smiled as he watched Ben take a rope halter and shank from a nail in the tack room wall, then walk up and down the barn's interior to pause before one of the occupied stalls, peer in, scratch his head, then move to the next and repeat the ritual.

"Five brides for the Jester." Ben turned to Sands and winked. "Which shall it be, Josh? Which of these lovely ladies will be the first?"

The brides Ben spoke of were five mustang mares Sands had bought for ten dollars a head while Ben was in Austin retrieving his thoroughbred stud, Jester. The mares were nothing special to Sands, just horses taken by Jack Hays's Lipan Apache scouts during a raid on a Comanche camp. However, the gleam in Ben's eye told him he had made the right decision in purchasing the ponies during his partner's absence.

"Does it matter which is first?" Sands said now, shrugging. "Every one of those mares will be spending quite a lot of time with Jester."

"True, but this is his first night in his new home." Ben grinned widely as his gaze returned to the five occupied stalls. "We want to make the Jester feel welcome here."

On the surface, Ben's concern for his—their—horses appeared somewhat childish to Sands. To the former slave, each horse was an individual, almost human. Yet it was that very concern that quieted the churning doubt in the ranger's brain every time he realized he had invested his life savings in this wild scheme.

Crossbreeding thoroughbreds and mustangs! I still can't believe I let Ben convince me to do this, Sands thought. At the same time, he recognized that his partner's basic premise made absolute sense. The frontier needed a new breed of horse—and they just might be the men to provide it.

"Ah," Ben said as he stepped over to the stall on his right. "This little paint looks like she's fit and willing for our new king."

At least Ben might provide that new breed, Sands continued to reflect. In truth, Sands doubted that his contribution to this venture would be little more than a strong back and shoulders when they were needed. If the Running WS Ranch were to thrive, it would be on Ben's knowledge—knowledge gained during an apprenticeship as a slave on a Kentucky thoroughbred breeding farm.

To date, Sands's sole contribution to the ranch, other than lending a hand with repairs and cleanup, was his suggested name for their spread—Belly Acres! The proposal hadn't even drawn an appreciative moan from his new partner.

"This way, little lady. Follow ol' Ben and meet the father of your children," Ben crooned softly to the mustang mare as he led her from the stall.

Sands followed the man and horse out of the barn. As they walked to a smaller barn about a hundred yards to the left of the first, they passed behind the ranch's single stone building. The ranger felt a touch of pride when he glanced at the low-slung, two-room house. He admitted that the ranch house, constructed of native limestone, was a far cry from a mansion, but its cedar shake roof kept the rain out, and the stone fireplace would provide welcome warmth from Texas' blue northers.

It was also the only house he had been able to call home since he had been nine years old. As crazy as Ben's scheme was, Sands found a security in the house, the land, and the horses that he had never known before in his life. A piece of Texas truly belonged to him.

He also admitted the sense of deep-rooted satisfaction he had felt while making the repairs to the barns and fences. That had surprised him—that a man could enjoy sweating so much. But then he had been building something that was his, at least fifty percent his.

I'll be wanting to plant a garden if I'm not careful, he thought cynically, smiling at the ridiculous mental image of a hoe in his hand. *Yet . . .*

He edged aside the disquieting thought that tried to wedge itself in his mind. *It's a good life,* he told himself firmly. *A man can make a place for himself here, maybe even a name.*

His self-assurances did no good; the restless disquiet remained, muddling the warm sensations that had filled his chest but a moment ago.

"Josh, get the gate to the stud pen, will you?"

Ben's voice drew Sands from his reflections, and he hastened ahead of man and horse to a square-built pen with a wall-like fence of pine rising eight feet into the air. A questioning snort came from inside when Sands pulled the wooden lock-pin and lifted the latch from its niche.

The snorting grew to an excited pitch as the sleek black stallion within sighted the painted mare Ben led into the pen. The pinto answered the greeting with quivering nostrils while Ben slipped the halter from her head and released her.

"No need for us now. The Jester can handle everything from here on out." Ben hastened from the pen, and Sands closed the gate behind him. "From the sound of her greeting, I think our little lady is in the mood for romance."

The former slave, now horse breeder, leaned forward and pressed his forehead to the boards, peering through a crack. "Lordy! The Jester is some horse!"

Sands's right eye found another crack and glanced in on the two equine lovers. A smile lifted the corners of his mouth, and he shook his head. While he couldn't compliment Jester's style, he did have to admit the stallion was a quick worker.

"Does Jester get another bride tomorrow?" Sands asked, glancing at his fellow Peeping Tom.

"Jester's one powerful animal, but he's not *that* much horse!" Ben laughed as he turned to his partner. "We'll let him and that little lady have a week together before we bring in another mare."

"A week for each mare?" Sands edged back his wide-brimmed hat in surprise.

"A good stud can get fifty mares with foal in a year," Ben replied. "Thought we'd divide up the Jester's time until we get our first Colts. He'll handle twenty-five of our mares, and we'll provide stud service for our neighbors for another twenty-five mares. That way we can make a little money while we wait for those first colts."

Sands nodded, then his head jerked around. "But we've only got seven mares, counting the two thoroughbreds."

"Which means we'll have to see if we can round up a few more," Ben said with a grin. "And we've got to find a strong mustang husband for Louisville Lady and your mare. Course we'll need another thoroughbred stud the quality of the Jester there. This place can handle more than twenty-five mares."

"Another stud?" Sands's brain raced. The Running WS had only been theirs for two weeks and already Ben was talking about a herd of more than fifty horses. As it was, it would be nearly three years before that first colt would be a two-year-old and ready for sale. "Thinking awfully big, aren't you?"

"We've got to," Ben answered with one of his flashing ivory grins. "But enough thinkin' for now. There's still enough sun left to make it into town before night, and we've got reason to celebrate. Can I interest you in a drink or five?"

"If you're waiting on me, you're wasting time," Sands answered. His thoughts weren't on bourbon or tequila, but on Elena Mazour y Chavela. It had been a week since he had last seen her, and it felt like a year.

Sleek, soft, warm, and supple, Elena's nakedness pressed along Sands's equally naked length as they lay in each other's arms atop Elena's featherbed. An hour ago, when their embrace had begun, they had nestled beneath sheet and blanket. Now the bed covers lay crumpled at their feet, discarded, as their passion provided all the warmth they needed.

"I like the taste of you, Joshua." Elena's full lips and tongue teased at his chest as she whispered in a low husky voice. "And I like the feel of you."

Sands's arms tightened around her delicate body while Elena's hands slid like heated velvet over his body. He felt the firm mounds of her opulent breasts flatten against him, stiff, erect nipples trying to dig into his flesh.

"When I was young, my father sent me to Mexico City to school so that I might be a lady," she said, her head lifting and her jet eyes rolling up to Sands. "The sisters there said that it was a sin to desire a man the way I hunger for you. I must be without shame, because I find no sin in being with you like this."

Sands eased her upward until his mouth covered those ruby-red lips and his tongue swept into the sweetness of her mouth. He knew the condemning words of preachers and priests who railed against the sins of the flesh. For him, those words had no meaning. What he shared with Elena was right and good, and threats of fire and brimstone could never destroy that rightness.

"Mmmm, so soon?" The olive-skinned beauty atop him wiggled, and her hips undulated suggestively as she felt his desire growing once again. "I think the ranch life is good for you, Joshua . . . and for me."

"Shameless wench!"

She laughed with abandon as he rolled her onto her back and pinned her arms above her head. His mouth ducked down to the creamy mounds that jutted proudly upward, his lips brushing one waiting crest, then the other as he spoke.

"Are you suggesting my manhood is flagging?"

"Not now," she answered with a little thrust of her pelvis. "But you have been less than attentive for weeks."

Sands glanced up at her, his hands releasing her slim wrists. Although he said nothing, his head nodded in agreement. He cradled her head in his hands and gently kissed her lips.

"It still bothers you, doesn't it?" Her hands explored the muscular expanse of his back. "Not being with the rangers."

"It's still there," Sands acknowledged. "The ranch and the horses help keep my mind occupied, but it's still there, eating at me."

Elena's head lifted from the pillow, and she tenderly kissed him. "*Mi corazon,* if there was something I could do, I would."

"You've done more than you know by just keeping me around and putting up with me when I get cantankerous." He smiled down at her, dwelling on the beauty of her features. "Any other woman would have kicked me out on my backside."

"I considered kicking this nice backside more than once." Elena's hand crept downward to squeeze his buttocks. "Sometimes you need someone to rattle your brain a bit."

"I'll have you know my brain still resides in my head!" He laughed.

"That's the nicest part," she said, "hearing you laugh again."

Sands resisted the urge to comment on "parts"—his and hers. "All it will take is a little time until I get the hang of being a horse breeder. Ben knows what he's doing, and I can learn."

Time, he assured himself. With time, ranging would be

forgotten. He *could* make a new life for himself; he was certain of that. All he needed was a little time to make the change.

Yet if that were true, then why did he feel that restlessness writhing in his gut? Why did he feel as if a part of him was missing?

Again Elena's head lifted so that her lips and tongue might find his. They did, with a hunger that matched Sands's own mounting desire. In that embrace and the passion of a man and a woman, he forgot about Ben, the ranch, and the rangers—at least for the night.

☆ ELEVEN ☆

Sands's hands briskly rubbed his bare goosefleshed arms to chase away the early morning chill as he stepped from the privy behind the Casa de Chavela. Overhead the sky was tinted with the rose and gold of sunrise. He smiled. Today would be a good day, with not a cloud in sight.

In a quick-footed trot, he hastened toward the open back door to Elena's bedroom and covered fifteen of the twenty-five feet before he winced as a sharp, needlelike prick bit into his left heel.

"You are feeling better, Joshua, to be dancing this early in the morning." Elena laughed as he came hopping through the door on one foot.

"The Romans in the time of Julius Caesar had indoor plumbing," Sands hissed through clenched teeth as he balanced on his right leg and lifted his left foot to examine its bare sole. There in the heel, he found the source of the stinging pain—a grass burr with three barbs imbedded in his flesh. Pulling the burr free, he flicked it outside with forefinger and thumb and shut the door. "You'd think in two thousand years we could at least stay at their level!"

"I was wrong. You're a bear this morning, growling and grumbling. Come eat breakfast with me."

Elena's eyes were bright and sparkling when Sands's head turned to her. She patted the side of the bed where she sat with pillows propped behind her back. A tray bearing a pot of coffee and a single dish heaped with ham, eggs, and buttered and honeyed biscuits rested on her lap.

"Manuel?" Sands asked, noticing that Elena now wore a very discreet, though very lacy black gown.

Elena nodded as she poured a cup of coffee and handed it to him. "He always prepares my breakfast and brings it to me in bed."

Sands accepted the cup and sipped. In his own way, Manuel displayed a quiet, subtle discretion. While the serving pieces on the tray were meant for only one person, the food piled on the plate was enough for two. Elena's loyal servant and bartender maintained the illusion that his employer had slept alone the previous night, thus protecting unblemished Elena's reputation. Although San Antonio might be an open frontier town, certain proprieties had to be maintained. Especially when it came to beautiful, unmarried women.

"There is bad news this morning, *mi corazon*." Elena loaded a fork with ham and eggs, then raised it to Sands's mouth. While the ranger accepted the offering, she continued, "Captain Hays is calling the town together at ten this morning."

"Hm?" Sands's eyebrows lifted while he swallowed. "What for?"

"Manuel was uncertain," Elena said. "Though he said there is a rumor of a Mexican troop riding toward San Antonio."

Sands's eyebrows arched even higher. "Who? How many men?"

Elena shook her head as she took a delicate bite from a biscuit, then reached for their shared coffee. "Manuel knew nothing more."

"I'd better dress and see what's happening."

Sands started to rise, but Elena's hand on his arm held him. He turned to her.

"Eat first," she said. "If there's trouble, I know it will do no good to ask you to avoid it. However, the least I can do is see that you meet it with a full stomach. Now eat!"

Hesitantly, Sands nodded and accepted another forkful of ham and egg. Elena was right—if trouble was brewing it might be a long time before he got another decent meal. Besides, if Jack had called the meeting for ten, there was no rush, at least not at the moment.

Sands's gaze slowly traveled over the faces of those gathered in San Antonio's main square. Beneath the taut, drawn expressions of both men and women, he could see carefully held panic—panic that might erupt in the next moment.

Not that he blamed them. What they had just heard from Jack Hays was enough to turn any man's—or woman's—blood to ice. Manuel's rumor about the marching Mexican troop had been wrong. The Mexican government was actually sending an army against Texas. The long-feared invasion had begun! Spearheading that force was a General Adrian Woll.

"How many are coming against us?" an unidentified man shouted from the crowd.

"I don't know yet," Jack Hays answered the faceless voice. "The messenger who rode in before dawn said that

Woll is leading over a thousand men. They will be here by tomorrow morning if they keep to their present pace.''

A low rumbling sound moved through the crowd at the ranger captain's pronouncement. The disquieted buzz might have turned into cries of terror, Sands realized, had it not been for the calm, cool tone of Hays's voice and his equally calm exterior.

''What'll we do, Captain?'' This from a woman to Hays's right with a baby in her arms. ''My man's off in Corpus Christi, and I've got four young'uns to look after!''

''My men and the town officials are now making preparations to protect the town,'' Jack answered, turning directly to the woman, then looking out over the crowd. ''I suggest you return to your homes and do the same. If you're uncertain about the safety of your own home, then take refuge at the home of friends.''

Again the crowd rumbled but was silenced when Jack raised his arms. ''There's nothing you can do by standing here. Return to your homes. You'll be contacted when and if there is a need.''

There were more whispered rumblings. Here and there Sands saw a few men and women turn and walk from the square, but the majority remained, still uncertain what course they should take.

''Go on home with you!'' This from a man in a black suit whom Sands didn't recognize. ''We ain't sure this General Woll ain't no more than another rumor. The Lord knows we ain't had nothing but rumors of Mexican invasion for the past six years. Until Captain Hays confirms a Mexican army is on the road to San Antonio, I intend to conduct business as usual, holding court in that courthouse over there. Which I can't do with all of you milling around. Now get on home so I can carry out the republic's business."

The black-suited man was obviously a district judge come to town. He was foolish if he believed Jack Hays had called a town meeting on a rumor, Sands thought, but the man's words had the desired effect. The crowd, still grumbling among themselves, dispersed. Sands released a long-held breath as they left.

"Josh!"

Sands's head jerked to the left at the sound of Ben Webb's voice. The ebony-skinned man pushed toward his partner through the remnants of the crowd. "Josh, what's the brass tacks on this General Woll?"

Sands shook his head and rolled his eyes to Hays, who now walked their way. "All I know is what I just heard. I was about to get Jack to fill me in."

"You two have just been impressed into ranger service," Jack Hays said without greeting as he stopped before the two men. "You and whoever else I can scare up will ride patrol with me tonight."

"Just like that?" Ben glanced at the ranger captain.

"Sorry, but I won't take arguments this time. What few men I've got are needed here in town. Somebody has to ride out and find General Woll and his troops, and you've just volunteered."

"Then this is no rumor?" With Jack so close, Sands could now see the worry on his friend's face.

"No rumor. We've been warning Austin about this for years, and now it's happening," Jack answered, easing his hat back from his forehead. "The messenger that came up from the south could only confirm that Woll was on his way with a full army of men. Which is why I need a patrol tonight. We've got to find this Mexican general and see what cards he's holding."

"Where do we meet?" Ben asked.

"Ranger garrison at five this afternoon," Jack replied. "Now I've got to find some other volunteers and do some planning with Will Simpson."

"Five at the garrison," Sands repeated.

"Be there on time, or the next time I see either one of you, I'll have your hides. I promise you that," Jack said as he strode away, leaving the two standing in the middle of the square alone.

"Six hours," Ben said. "That gives us time to ride out to the Running WS and give things a onceover before we have to be at the garrison."

"It gives you the time to ride to the ranch and back," Sands said. "I'll stay in town. I want to arrange for some guests to use the ranch for a while, if you don't mind."

"Elena Chavela and her girls?" Ben asked.

"If I can convince them to leave town," Sands answered. "Elena can be damned stubborn sometimes."

"Convince them even if you have to hog-tie 'em and throw 'em into the back of a buckboard," Ben said. "They'll be safer away from San Antonio."

Sands nodded. He was prepared to do just that if need be. "Meet you at the garrison at five."

With that, he turned and walked toward San Antonio's south end and the Casa de Chavela.

Sands hefted the last of the hastily packed suitcases and passed it up to Manuel, who stood in the back of the wagon. "That's it, Manuel. I'll go inside and hurry the womenfolk up a mite."

Sands turned and started toward the cantina's entrance. Surprisingly enough, Elena and her girls had taken little convincing to leave San Antonio. Manuel had been on the square for Jack's announcement and carried the news of the invasion force back to the Casa before Sands arrived. After Elena had seen to all her lunchtime customers, she closed the doors and began to pack. Knowing that she would be safely away from General Woll and his soldiers lifted a weight from Sands's shoulders.

"*Señor Sands*," Manuel called out. "There is something I would talk with you about."

Sands turned to see the Mexican bartender jump down from the wagon. "It is being said that Captain Hays is looking for men to ride with him tonight. I would like to be one of those men."

Sands's brow knitted. He hadn't expected this and wasn't certain what to say. He wanted Manuel with Elena and the other women.

"Manuel, I think it would . . ." Sands began.

"Would be a courageous thing to join Captain Hays," came Elena's voice from behind Sands. "If the captain will have you, then you have my permission to go with him, Manuel."

Sands scowled as he pivoted around to see Elena and her girls march from the cantina. His mouth opened to object, but Elena waved him away.

"Manuel can handle both a rifle and pistol. And on horseback there are few who are his equal. Remember, he was my father's head *vaquero* before the war," Elena said.

"But you'll be alone at the ranch," Sands started, and was once again waved to silence as Elena climbed onto the driver's board of the wagon and lifted the reins. Her girls hustled into the back of the wagon.

"Joshua, we are also capable of fending for ourselves," Elena continued. "I was born on a hacienda, remember? Manuel will be wasted in watching over us. And should you care to argue that, we could be here all day."

Sands wanted to argue, but the determined set of Elena's jaw and her narrow eyes revealed that she was willing to fight him all the way on this. Cursing beneath his breath, Sands shook his head in disgust. In an argument with Elena, there was only one winner—Elena. And he wanted her and the girls safely out of town before he joined Jack at the garrison.

"All right, dammit, but be careful!" Sands glared up at the beauty.

"And you, Joshua. And you, Manuel," Elena answered. For an instant her gaze drifted to the cantina. "I have left the door unlocked. Locks will not stop soldiers wanting tequila. This way, at least, I will save the doors from being battered down."

She looked back to Sands and Manuel. *"Vaya con Dios."*

With that she clucked the two-horse team forward.

"And may you go with God," Sands said softly under his breath while he watched the wagon roll away.

"She will be safe, *Señor* Sands. She is a Chavela and that is all that she needs," Manuel said.

Sands looked at the smaller man, suddenly aware of a fierce pride in his dark eyes. A loyalty to Elena that Sands wasn't certain he fathomed burned in Manuel's chest—the loyalty of a man who had devoted his life to the Chavela family.

"I hope you're right," Sands said with a last glance at the departing wagon. He turned back to Manuel. "Right now we've got to see about getting you a rifle, pistol, and a horse."

"I have all three waiting for me at the home of my friend Juan Ramirez," Manuel answered with a wide grin. "It will take me but ten minutes to get them."

"You've got five," Sands answered. "We're due at the garrison in fifteen minutes!"

The patrol was small, six men including Jack Hays. Sands wasn't sure whether these were all the men Jack could find or if his friend had intentionally kept the company small.

"I've only got one order for the night, boys," Jack said as he swung into the saddle and looked at each of his five men. "We travel fast and quiet. Any questions?"

He paused a moment, and when no question came, ordered, "Then let's hit the trail. There's a Mexican army out there waiting for us somewhere!"

Sands's heels nudged his bay forward as the patrol reined out of San Antonio and headed south.

☆ TWELVE ☆

Josh Sands dragged a hand over tired eyes, blinked, then stared up at the sky. The velvet blackness of the night faded even as he watched. Only the brightest of stars remained in the heavens as the gray of predawn crept upward from the eastern horizon.

"Damn!" Jack Hays slapped a palm against the broad horn of his saddle. His features were barely discernible in the murky dimness as he turned to his friend. "It just doesn't make sense, Josh! We should've ridden up on them about midnight. And what did we find? Nothing!"

Sands sucked at his teeth and shook his head, unable to piece the confusing situation together. The patrol had ridden a hard thirty miles along the southern road in search of General Adrian Woll and his army. There had been nothing. Absolutely nothing. Not a man or a horse or the crunch of boot on stone or the creak of a wagon wheel. All the patrol had found was empty night.

"Nothing! Dammit, nothing!" Jack repeated in frustration. "An army of over a thousand men just doesn't up and vanish, Josh. Somewhere, somehow, we've missed something. But what? And how?"

"We covered the terrain for a mile to each side of the

road,'' Sands replied as his mind raced in an attempt to recall something the patrol had overlooked. Nothing. They had covered all the ground, and there had been no trace of a Mexican army.

"Something," Jack muttered. "We've missed something. The messenger said that Woll was a day's march from San Antonio. That was yesterday morning. At forced march, his troops could make maybe forty miles in a day, maybe forty-five. We covered thirty miles of road tonight. Dammit, we should have run smack into his column!"

"We'll be back in San Antonio within the hour," Sands said. "Maybe after you get a little rest . . ."

The sound of approaching hooves silenced the ranger. Sands and Jack turned to the west. Manuel, rider and horse no more than a dark blur in the grays of morning, reined his borrowed mount down a bluff spotted with bushy scrub cedar. At a full run, Elena's bartender drove his horse to the base of the rise and rode straight toward Hays.

"The hill! Captain Hays, the hill!" Manuel shouted as he drew up, a shower of dirt and dust flying from his mount's hooves.

Jack didn't wait for the man to explain himself, but spurred the chestnut mare he rode toward the bluff Manuel had just descended. Sands followed at his heels with the rest of the patrol behind him in a scramble of rock and sand as the six riders crested the rise.

"Sonofabitch!" The curse rose from Jack's throat in a feral growl as he stared at San Antonio below.

There was no need for a telescope to get a total picture. All Sands had to do was look north to the myriad of camp fires that blinked and flickered about the town—the Mexican army had come to Texas!

"Surrounded! How?" Ben Webb muttered in disbelief from somewhere behind Sands. "How?"

"The bastard pulled a fast one." Jack spat in disgust. "The sonofabitch left the road and came at the town through the hills. That's what I overlooked! The hills, those damned hills!"

There was more than just camp fires below; Sands could see that now as the dawn grew closer by the moment. A city of white army tents encircled the town. And the soldiers! There were hundreds upon hundreds of those blue-jacketed and white-trousered uniforms.

"What do we do now, Captain?" Manuel's voice was a mere whisper.

"Nothing except wait," Jack answered, his words as tired as the face that was revealed in the rising sun. "For the time being, we wait and rest and think."

Sweat turned to thick white lather coated the bay's chest as Sands rode into the patrol's hidden camp and reined to an abrupt halt. As the ranger swung from the saddle, Manuel ran to the bay's head and took the reins in his hands. Elena's bartender then pointed to the right.

"The captain is waiting for you over there," he said. "You're the last one to come in."

With a nod of thanks to Manuel, who led the bay away to cool it down, Sands trotted to where Jack Hays sat atop a flat outcropping of limestone. The captain was bent over a map he had spread before him and glanced up when Sands climbed onto the rock.

"What've you got?"

In answer, Sands dug into a pocket of the buckskin

shirt he wore, extracted a folded piece of yellow paper, and handed it to his friend. "It's the same on the north side of town as it is here. Woll's soldiers are as thick as blue ticks on the shoulders of a coyote!"

"Expected they would be. We just had to make certain." Jack unfolded the paper and for a moment scrutinized the charcoal marks drawn there before transferring the symbols to his own map.

Watching his friend work, Sands lowered himself to the stone with a soft sigh of relief. Jack's earlier announced rest had lasted until the sun was fully in the sky, then he sent the patrol out again. Riding hard, each had circled San Antonio equipped with paper, bits of charcoal, and the orders to watch and write, or draw, what he saw.

"Thirteen to fifteen hundred men, is the way I make it," Jack finally said, looking up from his master map. "Damn sight more than a thousand, that's for certain. Woll came loaded for bear."

"Heard a couple of shots this afternoon." Sands pulled off his hat and ran his fingers through his light-brown hair. "Couldn't make head or tails of them. Probably just the soldiers taking potshots at rabbits."

"Same here." Jack pointed to the map. "This is the invasion we've been expecting. Look. Here, here, and there. Those are artillery units equipped with cannons, big cannons. Our General Woll's come here to see if he can take back a piece of Texas for Mexico."

"And we're only six men against an army." Sands's gaze coursed over the map. "The odds were better at the Alamo."

"Travis and his command were stuck in a run-down mission with orders to delay Santa Anna for as long as possible," Jack replied. "Our job is to tell the rest of Texas what's happened here, not to face the Mexican army."

"Couriers!" Sands grunted, making no attempt to hide his disgust. "Mexican soldiers have taken San Antonio, and we're going to be messenger boys!"

Jack looked up, understanding on his face. "There'll be fighting aplenty before we see the end to what Woll began today. But we've got to have men to make a stand. We do what has to be done now."

Sands realized that, but it didn't lessen the frustration. He felt like a man facing a herd of charging buffalo with both hands and feet hog-tied. "When do we ride out?"

"On the morrow," Jack replied, his gaze returning to the map. "I want more information before we raise a call to arms."

Sands snorted and shook his head. "Only way you'll get more than what you've got now is by riding into San Antonio."

"We'd attract too much attention riding in," Jack answered, his attention still held by the map. "I was thinking about going in on foot."

"What?" Sands's eyes widened as he stared at his friend in disbelief. "You're not serious? There's a Mexican army down there and a general who wants to walk right across Texas. A man would have to be crazy to even think about such a thing!"

Jack's head rose, and he smiled at his friend.

Mud sucking at his boots, Sands worked his way up the bank of the San Antonio River, crouched in the shadow of a willow tree, and peered into the heart of the city. Two blocks ahead he saw four souldiers with bayoneted rifles shouldered. To his right and left, other soldiers stood guard over the quiet, dimly lit, night-stilled streets.

Sands glanced over a shoulder and waved the others to him. From out of the darkness, Jack and Manuel climbed to the top of the bank.

"You certain you want to go through with this?" Sands whispered. "From the looks of things, Woll's posted sentries every couple of streets."

"We made it this far, we can make it to Bill Simpson's home." Jack's eyes darted over the scene before him.

Sands begrudgingly admitted that by half walking and half crawling along the river's bank they had penetrated the troops ringing San Antonio without drawing one cry of alarm from General Woll's men. "We were lucky. Damned lucky, Jack. You're pressing that luck right now."

"Then we'll press it. If we stick to alleys and take it slow and easy, we can be out of here by sunup." Jack nodded toward an alley to the right that ran west. "We're wasting time waiting here."

Before Sands could reply, Jack darted forward in a half-crouch and disappeared into the shadows.

"*Madre de Dios.*" Manuel's whisper was filled with awe. "What they say of the captain is true. He doesn't know fear!"

"And we won't know another sunrise if we don't get the hell out of here," Sands answered, running after Hays with Manuel at his side.

Slipping from one alley to another, the three wove through San Antonio, dodging Woll's sentries who stood guard on every other street. For half a mile a bone-weary ranger and a bartender followed a madman until he halted them behind a bushy shrub of cherry holly.

"Bill's place is across the street," Jack whispered, signaling his companions to crouch in the shrub's shadow. "Wait here. I'll be back in ten minutes."

Sands nodded and watched Jack dart across the street to a whitewashed house with the soft yellow glow of candles coming from one window. Jack rapped his knuckles against the window and was answered by the appearance of a man's shadow. A heartbeat later the window opened and Bill Simpson's arms were pulling Jack through the opening.

"He carries a heart twice the size of his body," Manuel said with obvious admiration for the man he now served.

"And the brain the size of a pea," Sands answered with a grunt, his attention focused on the two silhouettes at the window.

"Captain Hays knows what he does," Manuel said. "General Woll has yet to meet this enemy, but when he does he will learn to fear the name John Coffee."

"*Quien pasa? Levantese!*" A voice from behind them called for them to stand and identify themselves.

Sands's head jerked around; his temples pounded. His heart leaped, lodging itself in the middle of his throat. There, ten feet behind them, stood a Mexican soldier. His rifle, sporting a wicked bayonet, was leveled at them.

"My friend." Manuel stood and spoke in Spanish before Sands's brain accepted the fact that the soldier had managed to creep up behind them. "It is only me, Manuel Torres, and my friend Paulo."

"Into the light so I can see you. What are you two doing here? There is a curfew." The soldier ordered them out of the shadows.

As Sands stood, Manuel stepped toward the soldier. There was a glint of silver in his right palm as his hands started to rise.

"Tequila, my friend. We have been drinking and have lost our way." While Manuel's explanation held the soldier's attention, the small bartender's right hand snaked out, wrist flicking.

Sands didn't see the blade that shot through the night, but he did hear the familiar thud of steel slamming into flesh, the sound of a honed blade biting deep. An instant after that deadly thud, the rifle fell from the soldier's hands as he clawed at the single silver fang lodged in his throat.

Then Manuel was on him. Soldier and bartender fell to the ground. A blur of frenzied arms was all Sands saw; a rustle of two struggling men in the grass was all he heard. Then silence.

"Manuel?" Sands whispered as he stepped toward the two motionless men.

"I am all right, *Señor* Sands," Manuel answered, pushing himself from atop the soldier's lifeless body. "This one did not realize that he was already dead, and I only wished to ease his suffering by opening his throat. He will not bother us now."

"What the hell?"

Sands turned to see Jack come running around the cherry holly.

"It was nothing, Captain." Manuel bent to wipe his blade clean on the grass, then slipped it back into the wrist sheath hidden beneath his shirt-sleeve. "We had a visitor while you were gone. He said what he had to say, and I sent him on his way."

Sands smiled. Only moments ago, the small Mexican had praised Jack's courage. Now he had displayed a heart as large as the one possessed by the man he admired.

"Drag his body behind those bushes and let's get the hell out of here," Jack ordered, watching as Sands and Manuel each grabbed one of the dead man's arms and pulled him behind the cherry holly.

"What did Simpson have to say?" Sands asked when he stood.

"Woll's got a total of fifteen hundred men," Jack answered. "He plans to march on Salado before the week's out."

Salado! Sands's mind reeled. From Salado the Mexican army could strike anywhere in Texas—even Austin, capital of the republic.

"Simpson and the rest of the boys will be our eyes, watching every move the general makes," Jack continued. "Bill will send out riders with any new information he gathers . . ."

Jack paused and glanced around. "Hell, I said let's get out of here!"

Neither Manuel nor Sands protested as they followed Jack back toward the river.

Jack Hays handed each of his five men a folded piece of paper and watched them place the copies of his report on the Mexican troops carefully into their pockets. "Boys, I don't need to tell you how important what you've got to do is, so I won't. I just want you to be careful and keep your eyes open."

Jack then waved his five men to their horses and climbed

astride his own mount. "All right, boys, let's go wake up Texas!"

Simultaneously, six men dug their spurs into the flanks of their mounts and rode out into the darkness of the predawn morning, leaving San Antonio and General Adrian Woll's army behind them.

Sands lay low to the neck of his bay, the sound of pounding hooves and the wind filling his ears. In his mind burned the name written on the report he carried—Matthew Caldwell. He had no doubt Caldwell, a veteran ranger, would muster every man he could in answer to Jack's message. And when Caldwell rode, he would be at his side—their destination Salado!

☆ THIRTEEN ☆

With his hunting knife the only eating implement he had, Sands listlessly stirred at the tin plate afloat with pinto beans and bacon. The plate resting in his lap, the young ranger glanced over his shoulder at the yellow lights of the small town of Salado a half-mile to the north. The fineries of civilization might exist there, but not here in the Texian camp. Not even a fork or a spoon.

Picking up a lumpy sourdough biscuit lying to one side of the plate, Sands immediately dropped it in disgust. The bread hit the plate with a soggy squish; in the half-hour since Sands had been served the meal, the bread had soaked up the bean mixture like a sponge.

"Best eat the *frijoles, Señor* Sands," Manuel said from where he sat cross-legged on the ground on the opposite side of the campfire. Concern lined his brow as he stared at his companion. "Tomorrow there will be little time for food, I fear."

"I fear the same thing." Ben Webb, the light of the fire playing on his dark features, threw a worried gaze to the south. "Why do those bastards have to be so cheerful?"

Sands scooped a blade full of beans from the plate and carefully rolled them into his mouth, determined to eat

117

the meal. Manuel was right. This might be their last meal . . .

He edged the dark thought from his mind.

He had deliberately avoided studying the long line of campfires a mile to the south that had been ablaze since sundown. However, it was impossible to ignore the strands of guitar chords that floated up from General Woll's bivouacked army.

"You'd be singing too if we had as many men as them pepper bellies." This from Bill Simpson, who had circled the Mexican army with six men the moment Woll and his troops had begun their march on the small town. "Damned Meskins!"

"More than one *pepper belly* is sitting in this camp waiting to fight Woll's men." Ben glanced at Manuel, then to Simpson.

Bill's eyes lowered sheepishly under the reprimand. "Sorry, Manuel. You know what I mean."

"*Si.*" Manuel nodded. "I understand."

Sands's gaze shifted over the men huddled about the fire. Manuel did understand. Those Texians of Mexican heritage, though loyal to the republic, had slowly been relegated to second-class citizenship since the War of Independence.

Most of this attitude, Sands suspected, stemmed from those like Simpson who had immigrated to Texas after she had gained her freedom. They had not grown up with men like Manuel, seen them fight and give their lives for this land. The newcomers knew but one thing, the constant fear of Mexican invasion. From that fear blossomed an ugly suspicion of anyone with a complexion less than lily white.

"Wonder what they've been talking about for so long?" Ben tilted his head toward a fire about fifty yards to the right.

Sands looked at the ten men seated about the low-burning fire. Each and every one of them was a ranger captain, all gathered here in answer to Jack Hays's call to arms five days ago. Riding with them were more than two hundred men ready to face the invasion force that marched across their beloved Texas.

And we'll face that army at sunup, Sands thought as he studied the council of ranger leaders.

In the flickering yellow and orange of the flames, Sands could make out the face of Matthew Caldwell. Caldwell, along with the eighty-five men who had answered his war cry, was the first to come to Salado. His fellow captains had since elected him to command the motley Texian troops.

Sands would have preferred Jack Hays in command, but he had no doubts about Caldwell's ability and fighting spirit. He had briefly served with Caldwell at the Battle of Plum Creek when a ragtag Texian force had defeated the war chief Buffalo Hump and his marauding *Pehnahterkuh* army. The cigar-smoking Caldwell was as tough and durable as bullhide, and as with Jack, men were willing to follow him into the jaws of Hell itself.

Caldwell had been responsible for Sands's assignment to Captain Isaac Burton's Corpus Christi company a few months ago. Burton's unbelievable capture of two Mexican warships without firing a single shot had become legend within weeks.*

*The Texians #2, *The Horse Marines*

Sands could also see Ben McCulloch squatted on his heels beside Jack. McCulloch's reputation as a ranger stood without blemish. Tennessee-born, McCulloch had commanded an artillery battery at the Battle of San Jacinto. He had served briefly under Hays in San Antonio before becoming captain of a ranger company in Gonzales.

As Buffalo Hump and his Comanches had marched from the plains to the Gulf of Mexico, Sands and his friend Will Brown had served as scouts for McCulloch. Sands bit at his lower lip, remembering how McCulloch had used a small troop of men to nip at Buffalo Hump's heels, herding his red-skinned army toward that decisive meeting with Texian forces at Plum Creek.**

"Wonder what time it's getting to be?"

Ben Webb's voice drew Sands's attention back to his companions. His horse-breeding partner and now fellow ranger craned his head back and stared at the winking stars in the moonless sky above.

Easing his watch from a pocket, Sands thumbed open the cover. "Nine."

Manuel looked at Sands. "Is it always like this? The waiting? It eats at a man's soul."

"Always." Sands smiled with understanding at Elena's bartender. Manuel had faced and killed one of Woll's soldiers less than a week ago without batting an eye. Now tension drew his features taut. "The waiting makes the fighting seem easy."

"Travis and his men must have felt like this inside the Alamo, just waiting for the Mexicans to attack." Bill Simpson's head turned back to the line of fires to the south. "How many of them bastards are out there?"

**The Texians #1, *The Texians*

"General Woll's commanding two hundred cavalry men and six hundred foot soldiers," Jack Hays's voice answered the question.

Sands glanced to the right to see Jack and McCulloch approach. Matthew Caldwell now sat alone, puffing on a long, black cigar. The parlay of ranger captains had concluded.

"And I don't want to hear the Alamo mentioned again. The situation's not the same here, nor will the results be. We're positioned on open ground," Jack said as he and McCulloch squatted by the camp fire. "If need be, we can retreat, regroup, and face Woll again. Travis didn't have that option at the Alamo. He had to make a death stand."

"Besides, Woll ain't got that many men on us," McCulloch added. "We'll give him a scrappin' he won't forget tomorrow."

"Just how many men we got here, Capt'n?" Doubt tinged Ben's tone.

"Two hundred and eighty-five—every man jack of them experienced fighters and horsemen," Jack replied. "General Woll might have a few more rifles but he only has soldiers under his command. Matt Caldwell's got rangers!"

Sands bit back the words forming on his tongue. Jack certainly had a gift for understatement. Any schoolboy who knew his ciphers could have come up with the figures flitting through Sands's mind. Two hundred eighty-five to eight hundred made the odds near three-to-one—in the Mexicans' favor!

Nor did Sands want to confront Jack with the fact that many of the men who answered the war cry were like Ben and Manuel, capable men but inexperienced fighters. And there was the fact that Woll's troops had artillery to back them. When it came to a showdown between long rifles and cannons, there was simply no match.

"Captain Caldwell is certain General Woll doesn't know our actual numbers, what with so many bands of men coming into Salado from all directions," McCulloch said. "He wants us to throw up a little smoke tonight to help confuse things more."

"By the way, boys," Jack cut in. "For the time being, there isn't a San Antonio company; not enough men here for a command of my own. So we'll all be serving under Captain Caldwell. Understand?"

Jack's dark eyes moved over the faces of his men. One after another they nodded their acceptance of the change in captains. He then nodded for McCulloch to continue.

"Matt wants us to build as many camp fires as we can. Stoke 'em high and bright. Make it look like we've got three times the men we actually have."

Jack added, "He wants as much motion in camp tonight as possible. Wants Woll to see the silhouettes of men walking about those fires. So we'll sleep in shifts tonight. Half the men in their bedrolls while the other half make themselves seen."

Sands smiled. It was a simple charade, but one that just might work. If Woll thought he faced a Texian army equal to his own force, he might use caution in the morning.

"We'll face the Mexicans like rangers," McCulloch said. "Meaning we'll use whatever tactics and tricks we can, even if it comes to scratchin' and bitin'."

Jack found a twig near one of his boots and used it to draw a line in the dirt representing the Mexican army. "Captain Caldwell expects a cavalry charge the first thing sunup. We'll face that charge on horseback just like a spit and polish military unit. However, there will be a few surprises for Woll's men . . ."

Sands's smile grew wider as his friend outlined the first hand Matthew Caldwell intended to deal the Mexican invaders. Jack Hays wasn't the only ranger who had learned from the Comanches he fought.

☆ FOURTEEN ☆

"Easy, little mama. Everything will be all right, little darlin'. Ol' Ben'll see that nothing happens to his lady today."

Sands listened to Ben Webb softly croon to a dream. In this case a living dream—Louisville Lady. The young ranger glanced over the neck of his bay and watched the ex-slave slip a bridle over the chestnut mare's head.

"Ain't nobody gonna take my lady away from me." Ben lovingly stroked the mare's neck. "Ben'll see that you come through this without a scratch. Just put your fears away and leave everything to me."

Sands's head sadly moved from side to side as he threw a saddle blanket onto the gelding's back. In the fury of events that had occurred since General Adrian Woll's taking of San Antonio, he hadn't noticed that his partner was riding his prized mare. The ranger peered into the predawn grayness to each side of him, his gaze moving up and down the remuda.

It was a wasted effort. There were no extra horses to be found in this hastily gathered Texian army. The men who had answered the call to Texas' defense had come only with what they could carry in their hands.

Regret knotted in Sands's gut and lodged there as he lifted his saddle atop the bay. Today Ben placed a dream of a lifetime on the line—Louisville Lady. A ball of Mexican lead was just as likely to cut down the mare as it was her rider.

"Ben," Sands said from over the neck of his mount. "I'm sorry about the Lady. I didn't think or I would have tried to find you another mount. You're risking a hell of a lot riding her."

Ben turned to his partner, a sad little smile on his lips. "Ain't no more risk than any man here, Josh. Louisville Lady and the ranch mean the world to me. But neither one of them is worth a hill of beans unless a man's got freedom."

Ben paused as though listening to the creak of leather as 285 men saddled their horses. "Every man here knows that. Maybe I know it a little better than most. Louisville Lady and I will do our part to keep things the way they are."

Sands stared at his friend for a long, silent moment, then nodded as he drew the cinch under his mount's belly and tightened it. He then meticulously double-checked the loads in his rifle and Colt.

"Mount up. Pass the word along," Bill Simpson whispered at Sands's right.

The young ranger did. He then slipped his left foot into the stirrup and pulled himself into the saddle. With long rifle held in crossed arms, his eyes narrowed as he gazed toward the south, wondering what preparations were now under way in the Mexican camp. The light was still too dim for him to see anything but the flickering of dying camp fires.

"Sorry-lookin' lot, ain't we?" Ben's head tilted up and down the single rank of mounted men. "Don't look much like an army."

Sands glanced over the line of his fellow Texians. There were no crisp, starched uniforms here. In buckskin and linsey-woolsey these men lived and fought. Nor did he see high-topped hats with feather plumes. Coon and skunk-skin caps covered the heads of most of the men.

As ragtag as they appeared, Sands could not escape the ferocity ablaze in those determined eyes that stared southward. Each one of these men had cut a place for himself out of this wild and often soul-breaking land, and they would let no man or army of invaders take that from them. Today they were willing to pay the supreme sacrifice to protect each and every grain of sand to which they had laid claim.

Sands's mind filled with visions of the Running WS and Elena and her three girls who had taken refuge there. For the first time in his life, he understood the feelings that swelled his companions' breasts. Feelings he was proud to share.

"Sun'll be up soon," Bill said, turning to the golden glow that seeped upward from the eastern horizon.

"Hold your line until Captain Caldwell's command," Jack Hays said sternly to his companions. "Then we'll give General Woll a taste of Texas he won't forget!"

Caldwell's signal came with the first yellow rays of dawn. Without a word, his arm rose and fell.

Sands nudged the bay forward in an easy walk. A mile separated the two war camps. By sunup, Caldwell's plan called for the troop to traverse half that distance.

Less than a man's width separated each of the riders.

The tight-knit rank went against all the military rules, Sands realized. A good general would never place his men in such close quarters, making them easy targets for a rifle volley or a cavalry charge. But then, Matthew Caldwell was not a general but a ranger. The image of an ill-prepared army was just the image he wanted to present to Woll's watching eyes.

A half-mile from the Mexican camp, Caldwell's arm rose high in the air. Two hundred and eighty-five horses drew to a halt. Two hundred and eighty-five pairs of determined eyes glared at the enemy camp.

"There they are." Manuel spoke now, his tone low and tight.

Where's the cavalry? Sands's eyes darted back and forth along the line of soldiers in blue and white. Although there appeared to be no orderly military formation to the Mexican horde, they did have rifles shouldered. Had Caldwell and Jack misread Woll? Did he intend an initial attack with his infantry?

Seconds later, the disarrayed Mexican foot soldiers parted, opening a wide swath through which rode two hundred answers to the ranger's unspoken questions. They came slowly in four wide ranks of fifty men each, walking their fine thoroughbreds onto the battle plain.

Sands heard a voice bark in Spanish. A hiss like two hundred spitting serpents rent the air as the mounted soldiers answered that command, drawing sabers. Sunlight glinted and ran along those slightly curved blades as they rose for attack.

From somewhere came the booming of a bass drum. Sands blinked, recognizing the sound as that of his own heart pounding as the moment of truth drew near.

"Charge!" Matthew Caldwell's voice rang out.

The race of his pulse was forgotten as Sands slammed his spurred boots into the bay's flanks. The gelding bolted forward along with 284 other horses that raced head on toward Woll's first line of offense.

A Mexican bugle trumpeted, blaring its answer to the thundering hooves of the Texian mounts. Two hundred saber-bearing soldiers, war cries tearing from their throats, charged to meet the attack!

Sands could almost hear the swish of steel descending as he urged the bay headlong in a full run. But a cavalry-to-cavalry confrontation was not part of Caldwell's strategy this morning. Seconds before the two forces collided, Sands reined his mount to the right, as did half the Texian riders. The remaining rangers reined to the left.

The rank of ragtag defenders gaped widely, letting Woll's attack ride right through and past them. Shouts of surprise came from the saber-wielding unit, but it was too late. The Texians closed ranks. A blood-chilling cry screamed from their lips as they barreled down on the foot soldiers who stood expecting to witness Texas' easy defeat.

In the beat of a heart, Sands saw the shock, then the terrible realization sweep across those unexpecting faces. Those at the front, who had stood gawking but an instant before, now turned and tried to run. The mass of bodies pressing forward to get a better view prevented the retreat.

Twenty-five yards from the ocean of blue and white, Caldwell's voice roared again. In response, Sands yanked back on his reins, drawing the bay to a halt that sent dirt and stone flying into the air. A blink of an eye later, 285 long rifles lifted.

Ahead of him several of the Mexican soldiers fumbled

to tug their strapped rifles from their shoulders. Their reaction came too late. Texian rifles thundered, spitting death into Woll's disorganized ranks.

Without waiting to see the effects of the volley, Sands jammed his rifle into its saddle holster, wheeled his mount 180 degrees to once again face the Mexican cavalry that now charged toward him. Yanking the Colt from its own holster, he thumbed back the hammer, then again dug his spurs into the gelding.

If General Woll's mounted soldiers were prepared for the Texian ranks to once again open wide, they weren't given the opportunity to act. The instant before Caldwell's men reined to each side, the bark of pistols echoed across the battlefield.

Like every man in the charge, Sands aimed not at the saber-waving soldiers, but at their mounts. The toll of the attack was instantaneous. At least half the horses in the front rank stumbled, then fell in a tumble of flailing legs and hooves.

The riders behind the first line could not avoid the jumble of horseflesh and men suddenly thrown before their path. Man after man, horse after horse went down. Terrified screams filled the air and were joined by blazing Texian pistols as Caldwell's rangers rode by, emptying the barrels of their single-shot pistols and the chambers of their Colts into the panicked chaos that now remained of the Mexican front line of attack.

No victory cheer was on Sands's lips when he halted his horse a half-mile from the Texian camp. Nor was the thought of victory in the minds of any of the rangers as they reined about and reloaded their weapons. The sun still sat on the horizon; the day had just begun and many an hour lay ahead before the night once more cloaked the battlefield.

"Matt, to the left and right!"

Sands's head jerked up when he heard Jack Hays call out to Caldwell. There was a flurry of activity to each side of the Mexican line.

"The bastard's trying to get his men into fighting shape," Caldwell answered. "Let's see if we can delay them a bit!"

No ranger needed further orders. Caldwell had prepared them for this too. Again, the Texian ranks broke into two sections, swinging out to the left and right.

A war whoop rose from Sands's chest and throat as the muzzle of his rifle lowered and he rode down on the sea of blue and white stretched before him.

☆ FIFTEEN ☆

Sands dropped, hindquarters to the sand. Then his back rolled comfortably into the curve of his saddle for support. The sigh that escaped his lips sounded more like a groan as each muscle in his body protested the slightest movement.

"Son of . . ." The curse only partly escaped his lips. He was too tired, too bone weary to even cuss. All he wanted to do was lie here on the ground, secure in the fact that he had somehow ridden through Hell this day and survived. *I'm alive, and that's enough.*

Rummaging a hand into a saddlebag, he brought forth a strip of jerky. He sliced a sliver of meat the size of a ten-dollar gold piece, popped it into his mouth, and sucked at the dried beef, too exhausted to waste energy chewing. For a moment his eyes lifted to the night sky and the myriad of stars burning there, then his eyelids drooped gratefully closed.

"You should tend to that arm, *Señor* Sands." Manuel's concerned voice intruded into the ranger's drifting mind.

Sands's eyes blinked open, and he glanced at his left forearm. His buckskin shirt lay open halfway from elbow to wrist—a neat three-inch slice as though a razor had traced across the leather.

"It looks worse than it is, *mi amigo*." Sands studied the dark stain around the rent—his own blood. "One of General Woll's cavalry officers took it to mind that I needed whittling down a mite."

"I know," Manuel said. "It was my bullet that ended his life."

Sands forced his mind through the blurred fog cloaking it, attempting to recall the officer and his whistling saber. It didn't help. He had seen so many men fall this day, he couldn't remember. Everything lay hidden beneath a blanket of screams, gunsmoke, and crimson.

"Jerky?" Sands passed the smoked meat to Elena's bartender. It was all he had to offer in return for his life.

Manuel accepted the offering with a weary smile and began to gnaw at a twist. "Their guitars are silent tonight." He inclined his head toward the fires of the Mexican camp. "They are too busy burying their dead to sing."

"We hurt 'em today, that's for damn sure," Ben Webb said in a voice that sounded as exhausted as Sands felt. "They'll be lickin' their wounds all night."

Sands closed his eyes again to stem the tide of jagged images that tried to flood into his brain, unrelated sequences of death and dying. Later, when he was farther away from today's battle, he would ponder it and try to make some sense of the carnage 285 ragtag Texians had wreaked this day. But not tonight. Now all he wanted was sleep.

"Anyone heard a casualty report?" Bill Simpson's voice wedged into Sands's mind, edging sleep away.

"Twenty horses."

Sands's eyes opened again. Matthew Caldwell and Jack Hays stood by the low, flickering flames of their fire.

"Twenty horses, but nary a man!" Caldwell repeated. "Damn but we did Texas proud today! I've never seen fire coursing through the veins of men like I saw today."

"Wounded?" Sands mumbled, wishing everyone would go away and let him sleep. Tomorrow lay but a sunrise away—and with that sunrise Woll's soldiers would be waiting.

"Fifty men," Caldwell answered, "but not one that can't still hold a gun and fight, if it's needed of him. And I don't think they'll be needed. A courier just came in with word of a hundred men riding in from Austin. They're about five miles north of here. We've also received reports on several other Texian troops moving our way."

Any and all reinforcements were welcomed and needed, Sands thought. Today the men gathered here at Salado had accomplished the impossible. Not only had they faced General Adrian Woll's army, but they had held their ground, stopped the Mexicans dead in their tracks.

"The rest of Texas is just waking up to the situation here," Jack Hays said in his ever-soft voice. "We've got men coming, but we need more. I think you boys should hear part of the letter Captain Caldwell's sending out tonight."

Jack unfolded a piece of paper he had been holding in his right hand and read:

" 'The enemy are all around me on every side, but I fear them not.' . . ."

A wry smile touched Sands's lips. Caldwell stretched the truth a bit, but just a bit. Three times that day, Woll had managed to ring his soldiers about the Texian forces, and three times Caldwell had broken through the Mexican line of offense and sent the soldiers running.

" 'I will hold my position until I hear from reinforcements.' " Jack continued to read. " 'Come and help me—it is the most favorable opportunity I have ever seen. There are eleven hundred of the enemy.' "

Sands tensed when he heard that figure. Rumors floated through camp that Woll had called for reinforcements of his own, men he had left in San Antonio. Apparently those rumors were true!

" 'I can whip them on my own ground without any help, but I cannot take prisoners,' " Jack read on. " 'Why don't you come? Huzza! Huzza for Texas.' "

"And we can whip 'em," Caldwell now said. "We proved that today, men. Woll's bitten off more than he can chew, and he's just beginning to realize it. Another day like today and he'll be limping his way back to the Rio Grande wishin' he never heard of Texas."

Sands couldn't deny Caldwell's enthusiasm, but he did doubt the man's contention that the men gathered at Salado could defeat Woll's army. Fighters they were, willing to give their lives to stop the Mexican invaders, but there were limits to what such a small band could do.

The only thing that had saved them from defeat today was mobility. Time and again, Woll had tried to train his cannons on the ranger troops, but they had never remained in one place long enough for cannonballs to take their toll. If Woll had succeeded in surrounding his opponents, today's outcome would have been different—deadly different.

"You boys get some rest now," Jack said. "I'll wake you when it's your turn to take the watch."

Sands didn't argue. Nestling down on the ground with his saddle as a pillow, he tugged his hat over his eyes and slept.

*   *   *

"Josh." A hand shook Sands's shoulder. "Josh, wake up. Capt'n Jack wants to talk with you."

Sands batted a hand at his shoulder and rolled over, but the shaking and the voice persisted. He forced back leadened eyelids and looked up into the face of Bill Simpson. "What is it? I just got to sleep."

"You've been sawing logs for five hours," Bill answered. "Jack and Capt'n Caldwell want you."

Edging back his wide-brimmed hat and pushing up onto his elbows, Sands glanced to his right. Hays and Caldwell and five other ranger captains sat around a camp fire. "Don't they ever sleep?"

"Not tonight," Bill answered while Sands rose and dusted off his shirt and pants. "They've been palavering all night. Reckon they'll be there to sunup."

With a quick stretch to ease the kinks in his back and legs, Sands wiped the sleep from his burning eyes, then walked to the circle of ranger captains. "Bill Simpson said you wanted to see me."

"Josh, you rode courier for me a few months ago," Caldwell began as he stood and faced the young ranger.

Sands's eyes opened wider. He was surprised Caldwell remembered him, let alone his name.

"I need a good rider again tonight," Caldwell continued. "You and your horse up to it?"

"Both rested up," Sands lied. The gelding might be rested, but he felt like he had barely survived being trampled by a herd of stampeding longhorns.

"Good." Caldwell nodded. "Around sundown I got word Captain Nicholas Dawson and fifty men from La-

Grange were about twenty miles south of our position. They should have been here by now. I want you to find them and bring 'em here. We need every man we can rally."

"When do I ride?" Sands asked. "A friend of mine is in Captain Dawson's company."

"Friend?" Hays's brow knitted.

"Will Brown," Sands replied. "He rode down and joined Dawson's company about a month back."

Jack nodded. "Brown's a good man; we can use him here."

"Then I guess you'd better go and find this friend of yours," Caldwell said. "Just remember to bring Nick Dawson and the rest of his men along."

"Yes, sir!" Sands grinned. He might have wished for better circumstances, but it would be good to see Will again. "Give me a few minutes to gather my gear."

"Take two," Jack answered. "We need those men here now. Before sunrise if possible."

Sands nodded and turned. Five minutes later, he rode west out of camp, swinging in a wide semicircle around Woll's army before cutting south in search of Dawson's wayward company.

☆ SIXTEEN ☆

Sands reined the bay gelding to a halt. His head cocked from one side to the other, listening. Only the soft whisper of a cool predawn breeze and the stirrings of awakening birds touched his ears.

He cursed softly, certain that he had heard something only a moment ago. With a dubious shake of his head, he lifted the gelding's braided reins and started to cluck the horse onward. His tongue hesitated, pressed against the roof of his mouth.

There is something! He cupped a hand behind an ear, his head slowly turning from left to right. His lips set in a thin tight line. Whatever it was, it sounded like the clinking of metal on metal. And it came from . . .

Sands's head turned again, trying to locate the source of the sound. He sat in a shallow depression formed between four scrub-cedar-covered bluffs. The sound was muffled by the miniature forest as the noise shifted from one bluff to the other. *The east,* he decided.

Slipping from the saddle, the young ranger led the bay behind a stand of five bushy cedars. He tied the reins to a gnarled branch, then pulled the telescope from his bedroll. With another cock of his head to make certain of the

139

sound's direction, he scrambled up the rocky side of the east bluff.

The spyglass remained in his hand as he dropped behind an outcrop of limestone to peer below. The source of the clinking sound lay directly below him at the eastern base of the bluff, easily discernible in the morning's paleness. A Mexican artillery unit labored to position five cannons with their wide, round mouths pointed to the . . .

South? Furrows creased Sands's brow. Why would Woll's troops prepare for an attack to the south?

Metal hissed softly on metal as he extended the telescope to its full length. Lifting the spyglass to his right eye, he stared out to the square mile of open plain that stretched to the south of the bluff. His pulse tripled its pace.

Mexican troops moved in on all sides of the plain, attempting to surround it in a tight ring. Near the south end of the open stretch of flatland rode a company of mounted men, unaware of the trap that was closing around them.

Sands repressed the immediate urge to run down the bluff, mount, and ride to warn the horsemen. Instead, he focused on the mounted troop, hoping against hope. The array of coon- and skunk-skin caps confirmed his worst fears. The riders were Texians!

Still the young ranger forced himself to remain atop the bluff. To ride down carrying a warning would serve no purpose unless he could offer a route of escape for the trapped men.

The telescope lifted again, and he carefully made a circuit of the plain. There to the southeast ran a long hogback. To each side of the ridge were rolling hills. The Mexican soldiers stood concentrated between the rises and the hogback. The base of the ridge itself was guarded by only a handful of men scattered among the talus.

A humorless smile touched Sands's lips. Woll's officers had made a mistake. The hogback appeared to be a natural barrier, and under normal circumstances it might be. But in desperation it offered an avenue of escape.

Sands continued to shift the telescope around the plain. He found yet another gap in the Mexicans' offense. The western face of the bluff he now sat upon lay completely unguarded. In fact, the artillery unit itself lacked infantry to protect its position.

Slamming the telescope closed with a palm, Sands carefully backstepped from the bluff's crest. He had seen enough, and enough time remained to save the riders before the Mexicans completely closed their deadly ring.

Sands found the bay where he had left him tied to the cedar. Throwing the reins over the horse's head, the ranger swung into the saddle and rode the gelding around the western face of the bluff. Near the center of the plain, he could see the mounted troop of Texians, still unaware of the Mexicans who encircled them.

Spurs to flanks, Sands urged his mount forward, hell bent for leather. His hand went to his hip, intent on drawing the Colt holstered there and firing a warning shot.

There was no need. Three rifles cracked to his right. Sands reacted, throwing himself onto the bay's neck. Hot, angry lead whined above his head as the Mexicans' shots missed their mark. Again his spurs drove into the gelding's side. Another report came from behind him—a wasted gesture. He was well beyond range now.

The shots *had* achieved what he had intended. The Texian company ahead of him was alerted. As he raced toward the troop, the riders dismounted and formed a protective circle about their mounts.

"Surrounded!" Sands called out, drawing up before the men. "Mexican soldiers around you. You've got to make a break for it!"

"Josh?" Will Brown's familiar voice questioned. The eighteen-year-old ranger stepped out of the circle, walking toward Sands. "Josh Sands?"

"Will?" Sands blinked and realization penetrated his harried brain. This was the LaGrange company he had been sent to find. "Will, where's Captain Dawson?"

"Here, son." A bear of a man walked around the circle of men to Sands's left. "What's going on here? What were those shots about?"

Gulping down a breath, Sands hastily explained who he was and why he was there. "Captain, you and your men are completely surrounded by Mexican troops. You've got to make a run for it before the sun rises—before they can close in!"

Dawson, an inch shorter than Sands, scratched at a coal pile of a beard covering his face and glanced to the east. "Mite too late to make sunrise, son. Sun's already up."

Sands's head jerked about. He blinked in disbelief. The sun couldn't be up. But it was! In his race to warn these men, he hadn't noticed the steadily increasing light.

"And I see what you mean about them Mexicans." Dawson slowly turned.

A line of blue-and-white uniforms completely encircled the flatlands on which the company stood. With rifles leveled, they advanced on the trapped men.

"Looks like we ain't got the option to hightail it out of

here,'' Dawson said. ''Make sure your powder's dry, boys. We've got a fight on our hands.''

Sands's gaze darted to the hogback to the southwest. There were more soldiers now, but it remained a weak link in the Mexican offense. ''Captain Dawson . . .''

''Son, I suggest you get your horse in there with the rest of the mounts, and see if you can put that rifle to good use!'' Dawson cut him off.

''Captain,'' Sands started again.

The officer from LaGrange didn't hear or wasn't listening. Dawson turned his back on Sands and disappeared around the circle of men.

''Stubborn bastard!'' Sands hissed through clenched teeth while he yanked his rifle from the saddle holster and dismounted.

''He's a good man, Josh,'' Will said, leading the bay into the center of the circle. ''He can handle a couple of Mexican soldiers.''

Sands's mouth opened: he was intent on pointing out the fact that the company was surrounded by at least two hundred infantrymen. Instead, he swallowed his words and took a place in the circle beside his old friend.

''It's good to see you again, Josh,'' Will whispered as his eyes rose to the advancing soldiers. ''Sorry to ride out of San Antonio like I did, but I wasn't certain when you and Ben Webb would return. You two find that girl you were after?''

''Brought her home to her daddy,'' Sands replied, remembering the encounter with Forty Horses. Those few Comanche warriors seemed insignificant now compared with the closing ring of blue and white.

''Hold your fire until they're in range,'' Dawson's voice boomed from somewhere behind Sands. ''Then fire at will!''

"How many men has Dawson got with him?" Sands asked as he cocked his rifle.

"Fifty-three, counting rangers and the volunteers out of LaGrange." Will hefted the stock of his long rifle to his shoulder. "We rode out as soon as we got word of this General Woll's taking San Antonio and marching on Salado."

Sands nestled his own rifle in the hollow of his shoulder. His eyes narrowed as he sighted on the chest of a soldier directly before him. Fifty more yards and the human target would be in range.

Sands's eyes widened. *What the hell?*

"Captain?" a man called out. "Captain, they've stopped dead in their tracks. What's going on?"

The same question rolled through Sands's mind. Why had they stopped? What were Woll's men up to?

The answer came in a thundering explosion!

"Cannons!" A cry went up from the LaGrange company, but it was drowned almost immediately as the first ball struck the ground twenty yards from the circle of men.

A second roar came a heartbeat later. Again the Mexicans' aim was off, the ball exploding a hundred feet behind the circle.

"They've got us like sitting ducks!" This from Dawson. "Mount up, men! Charge their line and cut 'em down!"

A fourth cannon shot also missed its target. The fifth slammed into the southern portion of the circle just as Dawson's men turned to find their mounts. A man and his horse screamed as fragmented iron shredded vulnerable flesh.

"Mount!" Dawson screamed. "Get your . . ."

The second round of cannon fire began. Two misses

plowed harmlessly into the earth before the third struck dead center of the circle. The smoke and dirt didn't have time to clear before the fourth and fifth cannonballs tore into the helpless company.

Sands managed to find his bay, grasp his saddle horn, and scramble astride the frightened gelding. Beside him, he saw Will seated on a roan. Through the dust and smoke moved more riders.

"Charge!" Dawson called out.

Uncertain of the number of the dead they left behind, Sands did as ordered, following the LaGrange captain northward.

The Mexicans read their intent. Cannonballs tore into the ground before the charging line. Immediately, Dawson signaled a retreat. There was no retreat, only another volley from those damnable cannons—and death. Where fifty-four men and horses had stood, now there were only thirty-five.

"Captain!" an unknown man cried in horror.

Sands's head jerked to the right. Dawson, still in the saddle, clutched at a left arm that ran crimson.

"A white flag," Dawson said through clenched teeth. "They're cutting us to ribbons. Ain't got a chance against those cannons! Somebody get a white flag up!"

Somebody did. Sands's stomach sank. A white shirt tied to a rifle barrel rose into the air, waving back and forth for the Mexicans to see. Dawson had surrendered!

For an instant, silence reigned over the plain. Then Woll's officers answered. Five cannons thundered.

"The goddamn bastards!" Dawson's curse spat from his lips. "Make a run for it, men!"

Sands reined the bay around, his pointing finger jerking toward the hogback. "The ridge. Ride for the ridge!"

If anyone questioned him, their voices were erased as the whistling cannonballs struck. Men and horses, cut to a bloody pulp, fell.

"The ridge!" Sands cried out again.

When he spurred the gelding forward, the remainder of the LaGrange company was at his heels. Rifles and Colts were leveled at the uniformed soldiers who stood, barring the way to the hogback.

The Mexicans were prepared for just such a suicide charge. Rifles rose. Long muzzles carefully aimed at the yowling troop of Texians. Hammers fell.

To the right and left, Sands heard the terrible cries of brave men as death severed the fragile thread of their lives. Horses fell and riders with them, crushed beneath the weight of their mounts. Still the company charged.

Texian weapons answered the Mexican volley. Firing his rifle's single shot, Sands stuffed the weapon into the saddle holster, then drew the Colt. Three soldiers who lifted powder horns to reload their rifles died. The bay almost claimed a fourth beneath its pounding hooves before Sands reined the horse over the man.

Then he was at the base of the ridge. Spurs digging into the gelding's sides, he drove the horse up the steep embankment. Only when he reached the crest did he halt and stare back on those who followed. Fifteen—fifteen men of the original fifty-three—reined their mounts to the top of the hogback.

"Sons of bitches!" Tears of anger blurred the young ranger's eyes as he turned away from the plain.

More than half of Dawson's men had been cut down

after the white flag had been raised. They had been treach-erously butchered after they had surrendered!

"They'll pay for this, Josh!" Will Brown was at Sands's side. "Get us to Caldwell and we'll make them pay for every man they murdered today."

Sands didn't answer. Instead, he led fifteen men down the eastern face of the ridge. If these men were to have the chance to avenge their companions' deaths, he had to get them to Salado first. And at the moment he was uncertain if that was possible.

☆ SEVENTEEN ☆

Ducking behind an outcropping of boulders or a cedar break, hiding with pounding heart in throat while Mexican troops passed, then riding hard and fast. Thus it was that Sands progressed behind General Adrian Woll's line with the fifteen survivors of the LaGrange company.

From the north came the constant sound of battle—the sharp cracking barks of rifle reports, the thunderous explosions of Mexican cannons.

"Sounds like Woll's chewing Caldwell up," Will said softly as Sands led the men between two craggy bluffs. Will's young eyes darted toward the battle roar. "Wish to hell we knew what was happening!"

They would soon know how the Texian army stood when they reached Salado. *If* we reach town, Sands corrected himself. There was a question of his ability to get these men safely behind the ranger line. He had never seen so many Mexican soldiers, all scurrying back and forth through the hill country. Whatever was happening to the north was big, and all the Mexican activity indicated it went against Caldwell's troops.

"Captain Dawson's hurt bad," Will said with a glance over his shoulder to the wounded man. "Might not make it, even if we get help for him."

149

Sands couldn't fault the ranger captain, in spite of the fact he had lost the majority of his command. Outnumbered four-to-one, Dawson had bravely ordered his company to stand and fight. Even the white flag did not blemish the man's courage; horsemen are no match for cannons. Dawson had sought to prevent the useless butchery of his men. Little did he realize the depth of Woll's treachery. Even now, Sands's mind found it hard to accept the fact Woll had turned cannons on men who had surrendered.

A new volley of distant artillery fire rolled through the narrow valley. Sands gritted his teeth to contain his seething fury. Today Woll might reap the benefits of his cowardly act, but eventually he would pay for the murder of Dawson's troops. Texas had risen against Mexico once before and cast off its yoke of tyranny. It would do so again.

Sands's blue-gray eyes rose as he came to the end of the valley. A stretch of cedar and mesquite flatlands opened before him. For several silent moments, he sat studying the open country, searching for any hint of movement. When he found none, he turned to Will.

"We'll cut north here. Pass the word back to the men that there'll be no more stopping until we reach Caldwell."

As his fellow ranger conveyed the order, Sands drew a deep breath, then spurred his bay ahead.

Hell on earth! Sands's eyes ran up and down Salado's dusty streets as he rode into town at the head of the small troop of men.

Everywhere he turned were men—Texians in bloodstained bandages or hobbling about on crutches made from hastily cut mesquite branches. Sands diverted his gaze, unable to endure the lost, glazed stares the men returned as he rode by.

God! All this in less than half a day! He glanced at the sun, which still had not reached its zenith. If Woll's troops had managed to mangle Caldwell's men this badly before noon, there would be no Texian army by sundown.

"Josh, I think we've arrived too late." Will's head turned from side to side, his young eyes wide with horror.

"See if you can find some help for Dawson, then see about getting the men something to eat," Sands answered. "I'm going to try and find someone who knows what's happening."

When Will nodded and turned his roan back to the men who followed, Sands nudged the gelding near a woman kneeling beside a wounded man in buckskins who was propped against an adobe wall to the right. He waited until she ladled a tin cup of water from a wooden bucket and passed it to the man before asking, " 'Scuse me, ma'am, but could you point me to whoever's in command here?"

A face smeared with dirt and sweat wearily lifted to the young ranger. The woman looked at him with unblinking eyes, then shook her head.

"Should find someone down at the end of the street." The man with his leg wrapped in bloody calico lowered the water cup. "Saw Matt Caldwell headed down that way 'bout five minutes ago."

"Captain Caldwell?" An icy spike jabbed at Sands's heart when the wounded man nodded. For Caldwell to be here rather than on the front line only confirmed the worst of his fears—the Texian troops were being beaten back. "Thank you, friend. I'll see if I can find him."

Easing the braided reins to the left, the young ranger clucked the gelding down the street lined with wounded, where he found Caldwell talking with two other men Sands did not know. The leader of the Texian forces might as well have joined the other wounded in the street. Caldwell's shirt lay half torn from his body and a crimson-tinged bandage bound his right shoulder.

Caldwell turned and looked up at Sands. Noticing the focus of the ranger's attention, Caldwell grinned. "Ain't as bad as it looks. Mexican bullet bit a chunk of meat out of my shoulder. Getting it doctored gave me a chance to look in on things back here. Did you find Dawson and his men?"

Sands bit his lip and tilted his head in the affirmative. Sucking down a calming breath, he carefully recounted all that had occurred. Caldwell's visage grew granite hard as he listened to the report of the brutal murders.

"The son of a mongrel bitch!" Caldwell's words came in a throaty growl. "The bastard's getting his tail whipped, so he decided to take revenge on fifty-three men under a white flag. Believe me, Josh, he's paying for those men right now. When word of this gets out, he'll pay through the nose!"

"Getting whipped . . . paying for . . ." Sands stammered while his gaze returned to the wounded men along each side of the street.

"Don't let this fool you, son," Caldwell answered. "Five doctors came in this morning. I set them up here in Salado. I pulled all the injured men from the line. They need a chance at a breather. Most will be ready to rejoin the fight by tomorrow morning."

"Rejoin the fight?" Sands couldn't believe the ranger

captain's words. "Are you saying we've held against General Woll?"

"Held, hell!" Caldwell boomed. "We've got Woll on the run!"

Sands blinked, uncertain he had heard correctly.

"Sunup this morning, Woll threw everything he had against us! We fought his soldiers to a standstill, then pushed them back," Caldwell continued. "Then it was our turn. The devil himself would have turned tail if he were faced with a howling horde of angry Texians! Which is exactly what Woll did. The Mexicans are in retreat, son. We're just there hurrying them along now. Helping them find their way back across the Rio Grande."

Caldwell laughed when he saw the shocked expression on Sands's face. "No need to get down in the mouth about it, Josh. There's still plenty of fighting to go around. Woll might be withdrawing, but it ain't fast enough to suit me, or Jack Hays. You should see Jack and his company. I think Hays has got a piece of the devil in him himself. Jack and his men are nipping at Woll's heels like a pack of wolves!"

"Jack's company?" Sands's head moved from side to side. Caldwell was losing him with each word he uttered.

"Gave him his own company. Got enough reinforcements in this morning," Caldwell explained. "The Texian army is well over five hundred men strong now. And Woll's got a lot less than what he started with at dawn!"

Sands gave up trying to soak in everything Caldwell threw at him. He needed a couple of minutes to shift all the pieces in his mind and accept them. Although he did gratefully embrace one simple fact—the Texians were winning!

"Soon as you and the other boys grab a bite to eat, you'd best join up with Hays," Caldwell said. "As for me, it's time I got back to keep an eye on things. If I stand around here any longer, this shoulder's going to stiffen up on me."

Sands watched as Matthew Caldwell winked, turned, and mounted a dusty-looking black gelding that stood tied to a hitching post. As the ranger captain reined his mount toward the battle's din in the south, a grin spread across Sands's haggard face. *We're winning!*

Turning the bay about, Sands shouted down the street, "Will, gather up the men! We've got fighting to do!"

☆ EIGHTEEN ☆

Sands tugged down the brim of his hat, tilting it a bit to the right to shade his eyes from the harsh glare of the late afternoon sun. A humorless smile played over his lips as he studied the rolling country ahead of him.

Amid the rocks, prickly pear, scrub cedar, and clumps of pampa grass, the Mexican army steadily retreated up a lazy incline. Gone was the flashing spit and polish of their brass buttons and buckles. A coat of Texas dust and dirt soiled the blue and white of once starched and crisp coats and breeches. Only about half the men Sands saw still wore their high-topped, brimmed hats.

"Looks like they plan to camp on high ground tonight. And they've still got that bastard of a cannon covering their flank." Will Brown pointed to the artillery unit laboring to maneuver the fieldpiece up the side of the hill.

Sands's attention shifted to the cannon. The gun was big, a monster of metal forged in Germany and bearing the name Howitzer on its side. Santa Anna had first used such heavy artillery during the Texas War of Independence.

"Don't worry about the cannon. Those soldiers have their hands full right now. By the time they can bring it into play, we'll have come and gone!'' Sands spat a thin stream of brown tobacco juice to the ground.

Sands considered the cannon little threat to the ten riding with him. The artillery unit General Adrian Woll had placed to guard his backside had done little more than make noise with their Howitzer. The crew of men assigned to the big gun had a habit of overshooting a target.

''All right, boys, check your rifles and pistols.'' Sands turned to his companions. A grin spread across his face. ''Let's see if we can do some baiting!''

''Baiting'' was the correct word, Sands realized. For three days, the young ranger and the able survivors of the LaGrange company had devoted themselves to one thing—harassing General Woll's rear guard, a task they accepted with a passion.

Weapons primed and ready, the eleven riders urged their mounts forward in a loping gallop.

Bait we might be, Sands thought as he scanned the Mexican troops, *but there's a hook and line waiting for these blue-and-white fish. And a hell of a fisherman holding the pole!*

Sands glanced over his shoulder. Telltale dust rose from a deeply eroded gully a quarter of a mile behind him. That fisherman now prepared to give the fishing pole a quick jerk.

His attention returning to the soldiers, the ranger mentally gauged the distance between him and the exposed hindquarters of Woll's retreating troops. At two hundred yards, the Mexicans noticed the approaching riders. Fifty men in dusty uniforms halted, unslung rifles from shoulders, cocked hammers, and lifted muzzles.

So far, so good, Sands told himself in spite of the

increasing tempo of his pulse. *Fifty fish—so many for so little bait.*

A hundred yards from the waiting Mexicans, Sands raised an arm. Ten men reined to a halt beside him. For several heavy seconds, the horsemen sat staring at Woll's troops.

"Dismount!" Sands's voice rang out.

The Texians stepped from their saddles and handed their reins to two men assigned to handle the horses.

"Form your rank," Sands called.

Eight men fell into neat military formation, rifles leveled at their waists. On Sands's command, the line stepped forward. Ahead of them came the laughter of the Mexican troops. Eight men against fifty was suicide. The wide grins on the soldiers' faces plainly said that if these eight crazy Texians wanted to die, they would only be too willing to provide the lead needed to perform that service.

Fifty soldiers advanced to meet eight crazy men who were determined to embrace death this day.

With seventy-five yards separating his men from the Mexicans, Sands's arm once more jerked into the air, signaling a halt. The soldiers didn't wait for the ranger's order to fire. With battle cries ringing from their lips, they charged!

"Fire!" Sands answered the attack.

Chaos reigned. The men who squeezed the triggers to their rifles did so in panic. Shots went high over the advancing soldiers' heads or plowed harmlessly into the sandy soil.

"Retreat!"

There was no need for Sands's final order. His eight men broke rank and scrambled for their waiting horses.

However, the horses weren't waiting! The two men guarding the mounts fled, still clutching the reins to their companions' animals.

Behind the running men, the Mexican soldiers came howling as they tasted easy victory!

Fear and panic had sucked away the Texians' courage—or so it must have appeared to the soldiers who saw only eleven fleeing backs. Had they seen the wide grins on the faces of those nine men, an icy chill would have coursed through the Mexicans' veins.

During the past three days, Sands had lost count of how many times he and the men from LaGrange had repeated the scenario. And still Woll's men took the bait. To be certain, there were minor changes each time the charade was enacted, and it was played up and down Woll's line of retreat. Yet the Mexican general's men persistently took the bait—and the hook, line, and sinker!

When Sands and his men covered three-quarters of the distance to the gully, the fisherman who had thrown out the bait brought the hook and line into play.

With Comanche-imitating cries on their lips, seventy-five mounted men spurred their horses from their hiding place and rode down on the charging Mexicans. At the head of the company came Jack Hays!

Ahead of Sands, the two men with the horses immediately halted their flight. Seconds later eleven men sat astride their horses and joined Hays.

Realizing that they had been vulnerably drawn away from the rest of their troops, the fifty Mexicans turned and ran from the hooves thundering down on them. Rifles cracked and pistols barked.

Like shooting fish in a barrel, Sands coldly thought as

he emptied his Colt into the line of scurrying men. He no longer saw the Mexican troops as human beings capable of bleeding and dying. The moment those cannons had torn into Dawson's white flag, they had stopped being anything more than blue-and-white uniforms that had to be cut down unmercifully.

A hundred yards from the main body of Woll's army, Jack Hays signaled a halt. Sands tugged on the bay's reins and watched as twenty-five of the original attacking fifty soldiers regained the safety of their companions. The other twenty-five lay dead on the ground behind the mounted rangers.

"Move out, boys!" Jack's voice shrilled. "We've done all we can today!"

In answer to the command, the company spun about and rode to the north. Behind them came the booming thunder of a Howitzer, followed by the whistling flight of the cannon-ball as it screamed over the riders' heads, to end in a wasted explosion when the projectile slammed into the ground closer to the company than Sands liked to consider. A few feet shorter in range and it would have taken out several of the lead riders.

"Damn!" Sands heard Jack curse as he rode through the cloud of dust thrown into the air by the explosion. "One of these days those men are going to get lucky with that sonofabitch!"

Dropping his saddle and bedroll beside the trunk of a live oak, Sands sank to the ground with a weary groan.

"You sound like an old man," Will said from where he

lay stretched on the ground with arms propped behind his neck.

"I feel like I'm twenty-three going on a hundred and one." Sands leaned against the saddle and sighed. The ground felt like an overstuffed cushion to his backside after far too many days astride his bay. The ranger's nose wrinkled as the breeze brought a whiff of the evening meal to his nostrils. "Beans and bacon! Is that all Bill Simpson knows how to cook?"

" 'Fraid so." Will chuckled. "But he does it well. Beats the hell out of cold camping."

Sands glanced around the company camp and found Simpson busily dividing his attention between several skillets laid atop a wide camp fire. He moved from one skillet to the other, stirring its contents with a long spoon grasped awkwardly in his left hand. His right arm lay cradled in a sling. Two days ago Simpson had taken a rifle ball in the arm. Hays had suggested he go right back to Salado for treatment, but the man had refused to leave the company.

After cutting the lead from his friend's arm himself, Jack had pulled Simpson from the line and given him the official title of camp cook. Simpson had offered no protest. All that mattered to the ranger was that he would be there when Woll was driven back across the Rio Grande.

Jack Hays now sat with his two lieutenants, Ben McCulloch and Henry McCulloch, about fifty feet from Simpson's fire. The scene was familiar to Sands and had become the routine for the past three evenings. Jack and the McCulloch brothers would map out the strategy for the next day, then present their plans as the company ate.

Sands's gaze continued around the camp. He searched the faces of the men sitting or stretched out on the ground, gratefully savoring the peace of early evening. That peace was a deception. Less than half a mile to the south burned the camp fires of General Adrian Woll's army, a constant reminder of the battles awaiting the company on the morrow.

"Have you seen Ben Webb or Manuel?" Sands glanced at Will.

"Manuel drew early sentry duty," the eighteen-year-old ranger answered. "Ben rode off to the east after we made camp. Said something about having to do some horse trading before supper."

"Horse trading?" Sands arched a questioning eyebrow.

Will shrugged. "He didn't say anything else, except he'd be back around dinnertime."

Sands shook his head and rubbed his back against his saddle, easing a nagging spot of soreness. The four days that had passed since Woll's initial attack on Salado had definitely changed the face of this war. The young ranger had lost count of the number of Texians who now served under Matthew Caldwell's command.

The company had received word yesterday that all of the Mexican forces had been withdrawn from San Antonio and now marched with the main body of Woll's army. At least some of them did. Many never made it back to Woll's force. Jack Hays's men had seen to that.

"Beans and bacon again?" Ben Webb's voice came from behind Sands. "Don't that Bill Simpson know these hills are crawling with jackrabbits?"

Pushing from the saddle, Sands turned to see Ben riding into camp on Louisville Lady. Behind him were a string of five horses—all carrying Mexican cavalry saddles.

"What the hell have you got there?" Will asked.

"Longhorns," Ben replied dryly. "What the hell does it

look like I've got? Saw these five today, grazing back in a little valley carpeted in buffalo grass. Must have gotten away from one of Woll's remudas.''

Far more likely was that the horses' riders had been killed during a skirmish with Texians, Sands thought, but said nothing as he rose to examine Ben's find.

''Capt'n Jack was saying he wished we had a few extra mounts. Five ain't many, but I don't think he'll complain.''

''Three of these are mares.'' Sands looked up at the former slave.

''Noticed that myself, I did.'' Ben beamed and winked. ''Thought those three just might find their way back to the Running WS after we escort General Woll back to his home.''

Sands laughed. The face of the war definitely had changed for the ranch to be in the forefront of his partner's mind. Although the Running WS had never been far from Sands's own thoughts—nor Elena and the three other women who had taken refuge at the ranch.

''Captain!'' Bill Simpson called out.

Sands pivoted about to find Simpson pointing to Manuel and another man who walked in from the night. Simpson's excitement was directed at the second man—he wore a blue-and-white uniform!

One of Woll's soldier's he might be, but he carried neither rifle nor pistol. The first was slung over Manuel's shoulder and the latter lay tucked into the heavyset bartender's belt. Manuel's own pistol was cocked and pressed to the soldier's temple.

''General Woll decided to send this one out to spy on us, Captain,'' Manuel said with a wide grin. ''I found him hiding behind a cedar about twenty feet to the south.''

Jack stood and waved Manuel to him. "Bring him over here and let me take a look at him."

Bill Simpson left his place at the camp fire and stepped alongside Manuel as he directed the prisoner toward the ranger captain. The rest of the company pushed to their feet and moved toward Hays to get a view of their unexpected visitor.

With downcast eyes, the soldier stood as Jack asked in Spanish why he had been sent to the camp. The man offered no answer, but gazed at the ground.

"Answer my captain!" Manuel solidly tapped the side of the soldier's head with the muzzle of his pistol as added incentive for the man to speak up. "This is Captain John Coffee Hays. He has personally killed a hundred of your *compadres*. Talk or he will do the same to you!"

"Captain Hays?" The soldier's hand paused as he rubbed at his head, his eyes grew wide, and he stared at Hays. "You cannot be Hays. You are too small to be the Devil!"

Jack laughed, but Manuel replied with another solid tap of his gun barrel. "Why are you so concerned with my captain? Why does his size interest you so?"

Again the soldier fell mute. Twice more Manuel's pistol barrel was laid against the side of his head. The bartender's eyes flared with angry fire and his arm jerked back, ready to demonstrate what he was capable of doing to the man's skull without having to pull the gun's trigger.

"No!" The soldier cringed.

Manuel paused. "Tell the captain why you are so interested in him, and I will not smash your skull like a hollow gourd."

"The reward," the soldier answered. "I came to claim the reward."

Within minutes and without further aid of Manuel's pistol barrel, the soldier told his story. That very day, General Woll had placed a price on Jack's head—five hundred pieces of gold for the man who killed the ranger captain. The soldier had slipped away from his camp, intent on collecting that gold.

"Should I put this dog out of his misery, Captain?" Manuel looked hopefully at Jack when the prisoner had completed his story.

Again Jack laughed and waved off Elena's bartender. "Wouldn't want to kill off the only one of Woll's men who had the courage to come after that reward. No, Manuel, let's give him a plate of beans, then you take him back to Matt Caldwell for questioning. Matt might be interested in hearing—"

Thunder crashed!

A split second later Sands's brain recognized the exploding roar for what it was—the Mexican Howitzer! The whistling approach of the cannon's ball sang out in the darkness.

"Hit the ground!" This from Ben McCulloch, who threw an arm around Jack's shoulders, dragging him down.

Sands didn't question the order, but dropped belly down in the dirt, arms protectively crossed above his head.

The whistling ended in an explosion that threatened to rupture Sands's eardrums. The ground quaked beneath him as though the earth attempted to upheave and throw off the burden it carried.

Then there was silence beyond the ringing that filled the young ranger's ears.

"Everyone all right?" Jack's voice penetrated the ringing.

Sands pushed to his knees and stared into the darkness.

No one reported any injuries nor did Sands hear the moaning of wounded men.

"They got our supper," Bill Simpson said. "The bastards took dead aim on the camp fire and blew our supper to hell!"

Sands glanced to the right. A dark crater sank into the ground where Simpson's fire had blazed but seconds ago.

"Looks like more than one of Woll's men wants to collect that reward, Jack," Henry McCulloch said.

Hays stood and brushed the dirt and grass from his clothing. For a moment his head turned to the Mexican camp fires to the south. Then he looked back to his men, ordering several to stop as they hastened to cover the small fires that remained ablaze.

"Let 'em burn. We'll quietly move camp back about another quarter of a mile," Jack said. "Woll's men can have their target practice tonight, only we won't be here. Tomorrow, we'll take care of that cannon once and for all."

☆ NINETEEN ☆

Sands wiped at his burning eyes while he sat astride the bay gelding. He had gotten far too little sleep during the night. As Jack Hays had predicted, the Mexican artillery unit protecting General Woll's flank had sporadically fired shots into the abandoned camp well into the early morning hours.

Irony touched the ranger's lips; he looked up and down the line of eighty-six men who nudged their mounts forward through the furry cloak of a dense cedar break. Woll's soldiers would have the surprise of their lives this morning if they thought their random shelling had cut the company to ribbons. In spite of the price the Mexican general had placed on his head, John Coffee Hays was still very much alive—as was every one of the men under his command.

And as Jack had promised the night before, those men now intended to silence that damnable cannon once and for all!

Or at least remove its Spanish accent, Sands thought without humor.

The company of riders broke from the southern fringe of the break. Jack's silent hand signals motioned them westward. For half a mile, they rode silently over a terrain that grew more rocks and stones than it did either grass or cactus.

Here and there Sands saw a jackrabbit dart from the protective cover of a clump of pampa grass and scurry away on a frightened zigzag course, or a horned toad scamper hastily from the top of a white stone where it had warmed itself in the morning sun.

How easily the land recovers from man's intrusions, Sands thought as he listened to the songs of awakening birds. Although battle had raged here yesterday, the night had erased all traces of the conflict. The odors of gunpowder and blood had filled the air when he had fallen asleep last night. This morning only the flinty smell of heat wafted in his nostrils—heat mixed with the ever-present dust.

Again Jack's arm rose and pointed ahead. Accompanied by the clack of hooves on stone and the groaning creak of saddle leather, eighty-six men reined their mounts down the slope of an eroded gully. In single file, they rode eastward, following the dried creek bed.

Yesterday the same gully had concealed the majority of Hays's company while Sands and the men from LaGrange baited the Mexican soldiers into chasing them. Today the gully would serve as the launching point for the attack on the cannon.

Jack had selected the gully for one reason only—dramatics. As Woll's troops awoke and surveyed the land around them, they would be greeted by peaceful, serene countryside. A simple touch of spurs to flanks and that deceptive illusion would be transformed instantly, as eighty-six men abruptly appeared. One moment nothing: the next

a fighting company of Texians riding to the attack—
appearing from nowhere.

To be certain, the Mexican officers were now aware that
the dried creek offered easy concealment and the possibility of attack, Sands realized. Yet that knowledge would
not lessen the impact of suddenly finding a troop of rangers where none had been but an instant before.

Jack's arm rose, and the company halted, turning the
heads of their mounts southward. The ranger captain then
glanced to Sands and nodded.

Without uttering a sound, Sands eased the telescope
from his bedroll, threw his right leg over the saddle horn,
and slid to the ground. A single glance through the spyglass provided all he needed to know. A quarter of a mile
to the south, atop a gradually rising hill, General Adrian
Woll's troops stirred, readying themselves for the day's
trek.

Sands closed the three-sectioned telescope and scooted
down the incline on his backside until he was certain
he could stand without being seen by the unsuspecting
soldiers. Regaining his feet, he nodded to Jack and
remounted.

Still without a word, Hays lifted his rifle and cocked its
hammer. Eighty-five men imitated the action. Jack then
lifted a hand, circled it once in the air, and ended the
gesture by pointing southward.

Sands felt the familiar rush of his pulse, the pounding of
his temples as the moment of action arrived. His heels
urged the bay up the steep incline and then into a full run
when it scrambled over the top of the gully.

There were no battle cries. Every member of the company followed Hays's orders and rode in deadly silence.

Only the thundering hooves of eighty-six horses announced the rangers' charge.

That was enough. Sands heard the surprised cries of the Mexican troops, saw them running to and fro in a frenzied panic as they recognized the threat that had appeared from nowhere to shatter the morning's peace.

First to answer the Texian charge was the object of their attack—the cannon! Perhaps the Howitzer had been left loaded from the night before, or maybe Woll's orders called for the fieldpiece to always be loaded, but within the batting of an eye, the artillery unit swung the gaping muzzle of the monstrous gun downward so that it pointed toward the attacking rangers.

Torch was touched to charge. The pounding of hooves was drowned in a thunderous roar. Then there was the shrieking whistle of the approaching canister—

—and the fading whine when the volley passed well above the company's heads. Once again the inability of Woll's men to correctly aim their big gun sent a cannonball slamming harmlessly into the ground.

"With their first shot, let them know who you are," Jack had ordered his men while they prepared to break camp that morning. "I want to hear every one of you— eighty-five voices raised as one!"

Sands responded to that command now. From chest and throat, a battle cry ripped over his lips, rising to melt with the voices of his fellow Texians.

Blue-and-white uniforms formed a solid rank ahead of the young ranger, as Sands's spurs drove the gelding up the lazy incline. The barrel of his long rifle swung forward, ready to spit forth dead.

Sands saw the clouds of smoke billow from the Mexican rifles before he heard the crack of their reports. Above his head came a hot whine like the buzz of angry wasps.

The young ranger's lips spread in a taut, determined grin. Like their companions manning the Howitzer, the foot soldiers had lost their aim in the excitement of the moment. The rifle volley had passed as harmlessly above the ranger company as had the cannon fire!

Blood racing, Sands squeezed the trigger of the single-shot rifle. Fifty yards ahead, a soldier struggling to reload his own weapon jerked rigid, then crumpled to the ground. Beside his still body, blue-and-white uniforms fell like shafts of wheat beneath a honed scythe.

Somewhere to his right, Sands heard the cannon boom again, but paid it no heed. Instead, he freed his Colt from its holster and leveled it at a Mexican who rushed forward, intent on impaling him with a spikelike bayonet that jutted from the end of his rifle barrel.

The ranger's thumb yanked the pistol's hammer; his forefinger eased the trigger back. A dark purple hole appeared at the center of the soldier's forehead and a death scream tore from his lips as he dropped to the ground.

On all sides came the staccato reports of pistols. The air hung heavy, filling Sands's nostrils with the acrid stench of gunpowder. His companions fired round after round into the Mexican troops, and they fell, their bodies jerking and writhing in ghastly death throes as they fell to the ground.

Sands swung the Colt to the right and emptied another chamber into the chest of a Mexican who hefted his rifle in both hands to use its stock like a club. The man was dead before he completed his swing.

Woll's troops broke now, dropping their weapons and fleeing before the wave of mounted men who swept upon their ranks like locusts. Those who stood their ground died beneath the hail of lead the rangers unleashed.

Sands had ridden well past the company's original objective, the cannon, when he heard Jack's voice call for the company to halt. Jerking on the reins, he pulled his mount to an abrupt halt and sat watching the retreating wave of blue-and-white uniforms. His chest heaved as he sucked down gulps of air to calm the race of his pulse.

"Out of the line of fire, boys!" Ben McCulloch's voice cried. "We're going to give General Woll a taste of his own medicine!"

Sands glanced behind him. The McCulloch brothers picked their way over the bodies of the Mexican artillery unit to load the monstrous Howitzer. Easing the gelding to the left, well beyond the cannon's gaping muzzle, Sands watched the two rangers touch a torch to the gun, bringing it to thunderous life. When its canister struck this time, it was Woll's men whose blood ran crimson onto the ever-thirsty sand.

Sands felt something ease within his gut, like a taut knot unraveling. The smile that played at the corners of his mouth came not from pleasure, but from satisfied relief. Today the men who had ridden with Captain Dawson and been slaughtered while a white flag waved above their heads, today these men had been avenged.

With loaded rifle nestled in the crook of his left arm, Sands sat and silently watched the ragged procession. Later he would feel a sense of pride in what had been accomplished today. Now all he felt was drained, mentally and physically. Two weeks of constant fighting had left him an old man.

"They look different. You'd hardly believe they were an army." Ben Webb stared at the stumbling line of Mexican troops that waded across the Rio Grande back into their homeland. "It's hard to believe these are the same men who had me about to wet my breeches when I first saw them surrounding San Antonio. Lord, they look like beggars now."

Defeated men always look like beggars, Sands thought. Those who remained of the fifteen hundred men General Woll had brought into Texas were more than just defeated. Today they were walking shells of the soldiers they had once been. The constant harassing raids by the Texian forces had done more than break their ranks; they had shattered the Mexicans' spirit, crippled their souls.

"So many dead," Manuel said softly. "More will die in the long march back to Mexico City. They have paid dearly for their foolishness."

So many dead, his friend's words echoed in Sands's head. How many had actually died, the tallies of men who had given their lives, both Mexican and Texian, were the province of others, those who would sit with quill and paper in hand and glorify Woll's defeat. Their inked words would speak of death-defying heroics.

Sands shook his head sadly. Heroes had not fought General Adrian Woll's troops back across the Rio Grande. Ordinary men had faced the Mexican army, men who sought to protect the lives they had sweated to build for themselves in this land called Texas.

And as for death, it is never defied. The trail of blood

and bodies strewn across half this young nation gave grim testimony to death's constant presence when men faced each other with rifles in hand.

"It's over. That's all that matters," Will Brown said as he shifted his weight in the saddle. "We'll not be seeing Mexican uniforms in Texas again."

Several heads among the company nodded in agreement with the young ranger, but Jack Hays cleared his throat and said, "If I were a betting man, I'd give odds against that, Will. General Woll was sent here to test us, to get a feel for Texas' strength. We whipped him and set him packing. Now it's a stalemate, a standoff. The politicians in Austin will be eyeing the south, and those in Mexico City will be watching north of the border."

Jack tilted his head toward the Rio Grande. "That might look like cool, clear water out there. But it's black powder! Sooner or later someone's going to strike a flint to it and everything's going to explode. What we'll face then will make Woll and his army look like a church social on a quiet Sunday afternoon."

Sands's gaze returned to the river that formed the border between Texas and Mexico. Beyond the sparkling waters, a cloud of dust marked the retreat of Woll's troops. Closing his eyes, the ranger said a silent prayer, hoping that this time Jack Hays read the situation wrong.

"We've done what we came here to do," Jack said. "It's time to go home, boys."

"Home! Don't believe I've ever heard a sweeter word!" Ben Webb grinned while he eased Louisville Lady to the north, carefully leading the spoils of war after him—three Mexican mares.

Sands fell in beside Ben. He repressed the urge to glance back at the Rio Grande, afraid he would see a black river of gunpowder rather than the water he heard gurgling behind him.

☆ TWENTY ☆

Shivering in the early morning chill, Josh Sands waded from the shallow stream and caught the bundled store-bought shirt Will tossed at him. "I'm still wet!"

"Well, you can either stand there freezing your privates off or you can put that on and get warm." Will shrugged, turned, and strode back to the camp fire Ben and Manuel tended. "In case you haven't noticed, this isn't some Corpus Christi hotel."

The clatter of Sands's teeth didn't allow him to argue. He unbundled the shirt and slipped it over his wet body. He did the same with a stiff new pair of breeches, purchased with the shirt in Cotulla on the ride back from the border. A little water wouldn't hurt either; both would be dry by the time the sun was up.

Tugging on socks and boots, he strapped the holster containing his Colt about his waist, then perched his wide-brimmed black hat atop his head. He smiled, imagining the shock on Elena's face when he and his companions rode up to the Running WS. For once, he'd return from patrol without wearing half the trail on his body. `

"Feel like a new man," Sands said when he joined his friends by the fire.

"Smell like one too." Ben nudged Manuel and winked. "Just yesterday mornin' Manuel here was saying that he thought somebody had died and forgot to mention it to the rest of us."

Sands hid his grin behind a steaming cup of coffee and quietly bore Ben's gibe. In truth, all four of them had become a mite fragrant. The ride from Salado to the border had provided little time for such luxuries as baths.

Late yesterday afternoon four trail-dirty men had left Jack Hays's company to swing eastward for the Running WS. Anyone who had seen them camp last night and then seen them this morning, washed and wearing new duds, would have believed they had been visited by some biblical miracle, Sands thought.

"Will you be heading back to LaGrange, *Señor* Brown?" Manuel glanced at Will as he licked bacon grease from his fingers.

"Don't rightly know." Will tossed the dregs from his cup to one side. "I'd like to stay around San Antonio for a few days. There's the possibility Austin will let Jack bring his company back up to full force. President Houston has to realize the danger Texas is in."

Sands snared a strip of bacon from a skillet laid beside the fire and popped it into his mouth, chewing as he mulled over Will's words. Houston might recognize the threat Mexico presented, but that didn't mean the republic had the funds to meet that danger. As much as he hated to admit it, he was afraid there would be no change in the ranger policy. Like it or not, Will and he were out of jobs once again.

"You're welcome at the Running WS until you decide where you're heading," Ben said. "I'm certain I can find some chores for you."

"Might take you up on that—chores included." Will stood and glanced around. "How far are we from this ranch of yours anyway?"

"Two, maybe three hours." Sands drained the remainder of his coffee. "And we aren't getting any closer sitting here talking about it. Let's go home, boys."

None of his companions offered any objections as they rose, kicked out the fire, and walked to their waiting horses.

"I see no sign of . . ." Manuel glanced away from Sands.

The word he refused to say was "blood." Sands had searched for the same thing. All he saw was the shattered furniture. That was in the Running WS ranch house's main room. The single bedroom to the right contained a shredded feather mattress and a bed that had been turned into kindling.

What was missing was a trace of Elena or the three other women!

"The horses are gone! Jester, the mares—all the stalls are empty!" Ben was in a panic when he and Will ran through the house's sole door. "And the barn's been stripped. Not a grain of feed or a straw of hay. My God!"

The ex-slave's mouth fell open as his eyes took in the ransacked interior of the house. "Lord! It looks like a tornado swept through here."

"A Mexican tornado named Woll." Sands's lips were drawn in a thin white line, his voice low and dangerous.

"If he or his men harmed a single hair on *Señorita* Elena's head, I will have his *cojones*!" Manuel hissed at

Sands's side. "And I will personally see that he dines on them before I slit his throat!"

"Elena and the girls?" Ben turned to Sands, his eyes filled with unspoken agony.

"No sign of them. Nothing!" Sands's mind raced, trying to piece the terrible fragments together. The only thing he was certain of was that Woll's army was responsible for this. And if they had harmed . . .

Sands pivoted and pushed past his friends to storm outside.

"Josh," Ben called after him. "Where are you going?"

"San Antonio!" Sands answered without looking back. "If she's not there—Mexico City!"

"And I will be with you!"

He glanced to the left; Manuel trotted beside him. Fire burned in the small man's eyes. The same angry flame that ignited Sands's steel-blue eyes.

When the two swung into their saddles, Ben and Will ran after them. Four men ready to mount a private war of their own rode toward San Antonio.

Sands's simmering fury was transformed to shock, then befuddlement when he and his three companions pushed through the doors to the Casa de Chavela. He had expected the cantina to be in the same splintered disarray as he had found the Running WS's ranch house. Instead it was packed from wall to wall with men.

"I'll be damned!" Sands muttered under his breath as he stared at the scene.

"*Madre de Dios!* Half of Captain Caldwell's army is here!" This from Manuel, whose eyes went wide in disbelief. "What is happening here?"

Sands didn't know what to say. Only seconds ago he had been prepared to ride across the border to avenge Elena. And now he found this!

"We've walked in on a celebration, boys!" Ben grinned widely. "Our fellow patriots built up quite a thirst while they were chasing General Woll back to Mexico!"

Sands's head moved from side to side, still unable to believe the scene.

"Joshua!" Elena called over the din of male voices.

Eyes searching, Sands scanned the cantina but could not find the lovely owner of the voice.

"By all the saints!" Manuel sputtered. "Who is that tending my bar? Have I been replaced?"

"Nellie can handle the bar, Manuel." With a very unladylike swing of an elbow, Elena pushed through the crowd of men packed into her establishment. "Today you celebrate—all of you celebrate!"

Sands stared, soaking in the magnificent beauty who stood before him. Her own eyes rose to greet his.

"Elena . . . I thought . . ."

"Ma'am," Ben intruded just as Elena's arm started to rise to embrace Sands. "My horses, ma'am? What happened to my horses?"

She didn't answer. Instead she ran to Sands, threw her arms about his neck, and covered his mouth with her own. He offered no protest, but encircled the delicate woman in hungry arms, drawing her tightly to him. At that moment he had never felt anything more wonderful or more exciting than the womanly warmth of her body pressed against his.

"Elena," he began as their lips reluctantly parted, "I thought you had been killed or worse."

"I was afraid of that," she answered between a flurry of kisses to his cheeks and neck. "I wanted to be at the ranch when you arrived—had intended to be there, Joshua. But Captain Hays returned to town last night with all these men. They've been here ever since. It's like this in every cantina and saloon in San Antonio."

"Jester and the mares?" Ben intruded into Elena's explanation.

"They're safe." Elena's gaze left Sands and shifted to the former slave. "They're stabled in Nordine's Livery."

She turned back to Sands. "We kept a watch around the clock the moment we arrived at the ranch. Nellie saw Woll's men moving our way the second morning. We gathered our things and your horses and took refuge in a canyon about two miles to the east. There was a thick cedar break to hide us and plenty of grass for the horses. However, the soldiers never came near the canyon. We stayed there for three days, until we saw the Mexican army retreating."

She paused to bite at her lower lip. "The girls and I wanted to ride back to the ranch and clean up the mess the soldiers made of the house, but Caldwell's wounded started coming into San Antonio and we had—"

Sands cut off her explanation this time as he once more leaned forward and kissed her. His worries, his fears, all had been for nothing. He should have known that. A lady Elena might be, but she was no fragile china doll. A lone woman didn't survive on the frontier without a backbone of steel.

" 'Scuse me, but did you say, Nordine's?" It was Ben again.

"Nordine's," Elena answered with a laugh.

"Then if you two don't mind, I'll postpone the celebra-
on a mite. I want to go check on my stock."

Before either could answer, Ben trotted from the cantina
ith an ivory grin on his face.

"Will, please join the others. Drinks are . . ." Elena's
ad jerked around.

Neither Will nor Manuel was with them. Manuel had
anaged to work his way through the crowd and now
ood behind the bar, pouring drinks for thirsty men. Will
ood in front of the bar, demonstrating just how thirsty he
as.

"And how do you wish to celebrate your victory?"
ena looked up at Sands.

He nodded toward the arched hallway to the left side of
e cantina.

She smiled, started to nod, then looked about the cantina.
There are too many here. I am afraid, *mi corazon,* you
o will have to postpone . . . mmm."

Her sigh came as his mouth abruptly ended her words.
Vhile she nestled snugly against him, Sands swept her into
is arms and lifted her from the floor. Elena gave no
rotest, not even a disapproving shake of her head, when
e carried her toward that arched hall that led to her rooms
nd the featherbed awaiting them there.

Watch for

BLOOD MOON

next in **THE TEXIANS** series
from Pinnacle Books

coming in April!

EDGE

orge G. Gilman

More bestselling western adventure from Pinnacle, merica's #1 series sher. Over 8 million opies of EDGE in print!